D1025957

Dear Reader,

This Matchmaking Mamas story owes its origin to two things.

First, in a general way, was my ongoing frustration that I couldn't just pull strings behind the scenes in my kids' lives and find the perfect match for each of them. Happily, my son stumbled across the perfect girl for him and they are now laying the groundwork for their own personal happily-ever-after. One down, one to go. I always try to look on the bright side.

The second thing that inspired part of this story is the fact that during the course of my adult life, I have been in charge of taking care of the medical well-being of three out of four parents, so I can very much relate to the hero's feelings in this—plus I love to cook during those rare occasions when I have an hour to spare. So, channeling my feelings, I put together a story about a superbusy restaurant owner who became the man of the house at the age of ten, and a commitmentphobic doctor who seeks to fill the void she feels by being there for as many patients as she can. One of those patients is the hero's mother...and we go from there.

Thank you for taking the time to read my latest effort to entertain you and, as always, from the bottom of my heart, I wish you someone to love who loves you back.

All the best,

Marie

An Engagement for Two

Marie Ferrarella

HARLEQUIN® SPECIAL EDITION

Recycling programs
for this product may
not exist in your area.

ISBN-13: 978-1-335-46556-6

An Engagement for Two

Copyright © 2018 by Marie Rydzynski-Ferrarella

Printed in U.S.A.

USA TODAY bestselling and RITA® Award–winning author **Marie Ferrarella** has written more than two hundred and seventy-five books for Harlequin, some under the name Marie Nicole. Her romances are beloved by fans worldwide. Visit her website, marieferrarella.com.

Books by Marie Ferrarella

Harlequin Special Edition

Visit the Author Profile page
at Harlequin.com for more titles.

To
Charlie.
Bet You Never Thought
When You Sauntered
Into My Second Period
English Class That
First Day
That Half a Century Later,
We'd Still Be Together,
Did You?

Prologue

"Hi, Mom."

Maizie Sommers stopped short as she entered the ground-floor office of the real estate business she had lovingly nurtured and guided into a thriving enterprise over the last decade and a half. She was just returning from helping a young couple find the home of their dreams, something that always gave her an immense amount of pleasure.

The very last person she expected to see in her office, sitting in front of her desk, was her daughter, Nikki. Nikki, a pediatric physician and her only child, was responsible for Maizie initially dipping her toe into the—at that point—very unfamiliar waters of matchmaking.

She and her lifelong best friends, Cecilia Parnell and Theresa Manetti, had done so well finding a match for Nikki that they were encouraged to continue in their endeavors and find perfect matches for Cilia's daughter and Theresa's children.

When that worked out, they decided to continue matchmaking as an occasional hobby.

The hobby caught fire, and while all three women went on to maintain the separate businesses they had built over the years, matchmaking became very near and dear to their hearts—as was their determination to remain quietly behind the scenes. They were in it for the satisfaction, not the recognition—and certainly not the money since there was never any charge.

Maizie and her friends were quite proud of the fact that the couples they had brought together over the years never knew they were being skillfully guided to come together.

But that certainly wasn't the first thought that entered Maizie's mind when she saw her daughter sitting there.

"Is something wrong with Lucas or one of the children?" Maizie asked, giving her daughter a quick kiss hello.

Concerned, she dropped into the chair behind her desk, scrutinizing her daughter's face and looking for some sort of indication as to what had brought Nikki here in the middle of the day.

"What makes you think there's something wrong with one of them?" Nikki asked.

"Well, let me see. You're a highly regarded pediatrician whose hours are only slightly shorter than God's. You're a wife and the mother of three very energetic young children. That alone uses up every moment of your day and night, and I haven't seen you since Ellie and Addie's party," Maizie reminded her, mentioning the twins' fourth birthday last month. "My guess is that only an emergency of some sort would bring you here to see me in the middle of the day."

Nikki sat up a little straighter in the chair, although she was unconsciously knotting her fingers together. "Well, you're wrong."

Maizie continued to watch her daughter's hands. "Good."

"It's not an emergency," Nikki emphasized.

"Happy to hear that." Although, Maizie thought, something was definitely wrong. Those were not the hands of a carefree, untroubled person.

"Not exactly," Nikki amended.

"Ah." Now they were getting to it, Maizie thought. "And what is it, exactly?" she asked her daughter.

Just then her phone rang.

Nikki looked at the landline on her mother's desk. "You want to get that?" she asked.

"No," Maizie answered. She didn't want her daughter using the call as an excuse to suddenly change her mind and leave. "That's why God created answering machines."

Nikki appeared guilty. "I feel bad, taking up your time like this." She looked at the phone. The call had obviously gone to voice mail. "You worked really hard to get here."

"One delayed call isn't going to torpedo my business, Nikki. Besides, Susanna, my assistant, is due back from lunch soon. She can call whoever it is back. You are, and always have been, my first priority," Maizie insisted. "I've expanded that to include Lucas and the children, but you are still in first place. Now, what's this all about? And why are you about to twist off your fingers?" She nodded at her daughter's hands.

Stilling her hands, Nikki sighed. "I don't quite know how to say this, Mom."

"One word at a time is usually the way to do it," Maizie encouraged. "At this point in my life I've heard just about everything," she added, "so just spit it out, my love."

"I know—" Nikki began and then she paused, at a loss how to continue.

"You know what, dear?" Maizie asked, waiting.

Nikki took a breath, then blurted it out. "That you arranged to bring Lucas and me together."

Maizie smiled. She was surprised that it had taken Nikki so long to come to this conclusion. "I see. Well, those were just the circumstances that arranged themselves, dear."

"That you took advantage of," Nikki said, knowing the way her mother operated.

Maizie tried to understand what her daughter was getting at. "You're not telling me that, after all these years of marital bliss, you're going to get upset with me for meddling in your life, are you?"

Untangling her fingers, Nikki gripped the chair's armrests to keep her hands apart. "No, I'm not."

"Well, I'm glad we cleared that up." Maizie smiled at her. "Anything else?"

Nikki still hadn't gotten to the reason she was here. "Yes, um…"

"Go ahead, dear," Maizie urged patiently.

"I need you to meddle again, Mom."

"You're looking for another husband?" Maizie asked wryly.

Nikki's eyes widened. For a moment, she didn't realize that her mother was kidding. "No!"

"Good, because I really do like Lucas." Still smiling, Maizie became serious. "Talk to me, Nikki," she encouraged. "It never used to be this hard for us to talk. What's on your mind?"

Nikki decided to choose a roundabout approach instead of being direct. "Do you remember my friend Michelle McKenna?"

"Mikki? Of course I remember her. Lovely girl. Not the best parents," Maizie recalled, "but a lovely girl. She was over at the house a lot when you were younger and you two went to medical school together," she said to prove that she really did remember the girl. "What about her?"

"I want you to do for her what you did for me," Nikki said.

Ah, now it was all beginning to make sense, Maizie thought. "Does she know you're asking me to…matchmake?" Maizie asked tactfully.

"Oh, no, no, and I don't want her to know," Nikki said with feeling. "She'd never agree to it."

Maizie was well acquainted with that sort of reaction. "Why would you want me to do it, then?"

"Because she's a wonderful person, Mom," Nikki cried. "And she deserves to be happy. But I'm worried she's going to wind up alone. She's so afraid of making her mother's mistakes, she won't even think about going out with anyone."

Maizie looked at her daughter thoughtfully. She was well aware of the other young woman's situation. Mikki's parents had fought constantly and then went through a vicious divorce when she was a preteen. Her mother went on to marry—and divorce—three more times. She had no idea how many times Mikki's father had gone that route. The man had dropped out of sight, from what she gathered.

What she did know was that all this had taken a heavy toll on the young woman. She'd had Mikki stay over for sleepovers as often as she could to spare her daughter's friend from witnessing the acrimony manifested by her parents.

"Will you do it, Mom? Will you work your magic for Mikki?" Nikki asked her.

Maizie was more than happy to help. "Yes, of course I will. On one condition, though," she added, eyeing her daughter.

"What?" Nikki asked.

"You tell me how you found out that I had a hand in bringing you and Lucas together."

Nikki laughed, relieved. "You mean other than the fact that I'm brilliant, like my mother?"

Maizie smiled. "Yes, other than that."

"Jewel figured it out and told me," Nikki answered. Jewel was Cilia's daughter and she, like Theresa's two offspring, was Nikki's friend.

"I see." She nodded, accepting the explanation at face value. "All right then, I'm going to need some current information about Mikki—it's been a while since I've seen her," Maizie told her daughter. And then she smiled. "Don't worry, this'll be painless, and Mikki will never know that you came to me—unless you want her to know," she qualified.

"Heaven forbid," Nikki cried. Then, in a more subdued voice, she asked, "Will you let me know who you pick out?"

Maizie smiled mysteriously. She knew it would be for the best if her daughter remained in the dark until the proper meeting was arranged and pulled off.

"Oh, darling, a magician never reveals her secrets," Maizie told her daughter with a wink.

Chapter One

"There's someone to see you, Mrs. Manetti."

Melinda Jacobsen's announcement as she peered into Theresa's back office was accompanied by a giggle best suited to the teenager she'd been eight years ago when she had first come to work for Theresa's catering company in an apprentice capacity.

Theresa jotted down a last-minute thought about a menu she was creating in her notebook and then looked up.

"Bring her in, Melinda," Theresa told the young woman whom she'd eventually placed in charge of baked goods.

Hearing Melinda giggle again, Theresa wondered what had come over her. Melinda was usually very level-headed.

"It's a *he*." This time the giggle came before the words, further arousing Theresa's curiosity.

In less than ten seconds, her curiosity was laid to rest. Jeff Sabatino stepped around Melinda and entered the small, crowded office where she took her calls and created the menus that made her catering business such a prosperous success.

As if reading her mind, the young woman reluctantly left the room before Theresa could ask her to leave.

The tall, broad-shouldered man with thick, slightly unruly dark hair smiled at his former boss. "Hello, Mrs. Manetti. I hope you don't mind my stopping by without calling first."

Jeff had gotten his start with Theresa's catering business before branching out and opening his own restaurant a handful of years ago. Theresa had been one of his first customers and was proud of his success. She had always thought of him as a protégé.

"Of course I don't mind. And Jeff, you own your own restaurant, and I saw that you've been getting some really stunning reviews lately. I think you can call me Theresa now," she told him warmly. Theresa gestured toward the two chairs that were facing her desk, the ones where clients usually sat when they came to engage her services. "Please, sit."

"That's all right," Jeff told her. "I'm not staying long."

"Looking to buy me out?" Theresa asked with a trace of amusement. She knew that wasn't the case, but Jeff appeared way too serious for this to be strictly a social call. "Or are you here because you need help—because your restaurant is doing so well, you find that you just can't keep up with the demand?"

"Neither," Jeff answered, "although I'll never forget the debt I owe you. I would have been nothing more than a short-order cook if it hadn't been for what you taught me."

Theresa thought back to when he'd first walked into her establishment, a very handsome, very nervous young man with a great deal of promise. The memory warmed her heart and made her smile.

"Ah, but you had the *potential* to do so much more than that, and you wanted to learn. Desire is something I can't teach, Jeff. Everything else, I can." She assessed him more closely as she stood. She saw worry in his light green eyes. "This isn't a social call, is it, Jeff?"

"Not exactly," Jeff confessed.

Theresa made her way behind him to the door of her office and closed it. She had a feeling her former protégé would prefer privacy.

Turning around to face him, she said, "I'm listening."

Now that he was here, Jeff wasn't sure how to start. He wasn't in the habit of asking for favors, especially not from the woman he credited with giving him not only his start, but also the push to open his own restaurant— not to mention that she had also lent him the money to get started.

He'd paid off the latter, but in his heart, he would forever be in Theresa Manetti's debt. Which made coming here, hat in hand, rather awkward for him.

But this wasn't for him, Jeff reminded himself. It was for his mother. Thinking of that now, he pushed on. "I remember that you once said one of your close friends has a daughter who's a doctor."

"I might have mentioned it," Theresa recalled. "And if I did, I was talking about Maizie. Her daughter, Nikki, is a doctor." A slight note of confusion entered her voice. "But Nikki's a pediatrician and I don't imagine that you're looking for a baby doctor—are you?" she asked suddenly, looking at him in surprise.

It had been a while since she'd been in contact with Jeff, and although she would have liked to think he would have gotten in touch to tell her if he was getting married, she really had no guarantee of that. After all, he was a very busy young man these days.

"No," Jeff quickly answered. "But your friend's daughter does interact with other doctors, doesn't she?" he asked. "At the hospital, I mean."

She wasn't accustomed to seeing Jeff this unsure of himself, not since he'd first come to work for her. She tried to set him at ease.

"Nikki's a very friendly young woman, so yes, I'm sure she does. What's this all about, Jeff? Are you ill?" she asked, displaying a deeply ingrained mother's sense of concern.

He suddenly realized how he had to be coming across. "Oh, no, not me—"

"Your wife, then?" she asked, watching his face to see if she'd guessed correctly.

"No, no wife. No time," Jeff added, then told her, "You know I'd never get married without inviting you, Mrs. Man—Theresa," he corrected before she could. "You're like a second mother to me." He sighed. "Which brings me to my first mother."

"Your mother's ill?" Theresa asked, recalling how supportive the woman had been of her son when he'd first opened his restaurant, Dinner for Two. "What's wrong, Jeff?"

"That's why I need the name of a good doctor—preferably one with a really good bedside manner about him—or her," he added quickly. "Actually, I think my mother would prefer a her," he told Theresa. "As for me, I'd just prefer a good doctor."

"When was the last time your mother saw a doctor?" Theresa asked, curious.

He really didn't have to stop to think. He knew. His mother avoided doctors as if they carried the plague in their pocket. "When she gave birth to my sister. Tina's twenty-nine now," he added.

That was really hard to believe. "You're kidding," Theresa said.

"No, I'm not," he said honestly. "My mother doesn't trust doctors. A doctor misdiagnosed my father's condition until it was too late to save him." It had happened twenty-five years ago. At the age of ten, he'd suddenly been the man of the family. "He died."

"I'm very sorry to hear that," Theresa said with genuine sympathy. "But that doesn't mean all doctors are like that."

He blew out a breath, feeling very weary all of a sudden. "I know that, but my mother, well, it's hard to win an argument with her. However, she's getting weaker and I just might be able to bully her into it—if I can find a competent, sympathetic doctor to take my mother to."

"Which is where I come in," Theresa concluded.

Jeff nodded. "Could you put me in contact with your friend's daughter? Or have your friend's daughter recommend someone to you? I don't care how it's done," he told her, feeling just a little desperate, as if he was fighting the clock.

He had no idea just how serious his mother's condition was, but she'd been in pain recently. A lot of pain. "I just need it done. I'll take my mother to see this doctor on your say-so. My mom's only sixty-five, Theresa, and she has a lot of life left—as long as I can get her to see reason and get treatment for whatever it is that's making her feel so weak and ill."

Theresa smiled at him. She found his concern for his mother touching.

"You're a good son, Jeff," she told him affectionately.

Jeff shrugged away the compliment. He appreciated what Theresa was saying, but he really needed the name of that doctor. "She's a good mother. I'd like her to live long enough to see her grandkids."

Theresa's ears perked up. "So there is something I should know about?"

Jeff laughed softly. "My sister, Tina, has got two kids and my brother's wife is two months away from giving birth to their first baby."

Since he'd opened the door, Theresa saw no reason not to slip in and satisfy her curiosity. "What about you, Jeff? Would you like to have children?"

It wasn't something he thought about often. "First I'd have to find a wife who would be willing to put up with my crazy hours—"

Theresa's antennae went up a little higher. "But if you did?" she pressed.

"Then yes, I guess I'd like to have kids," he allowed. "But right now, I just want to find someone who can get my mom well."

Theresa nodded. "I'm on it," she told the young man she thought of as a son. "Consider it already taken care of, Jeff," she added with a smile.

He paused to kiss her cheek before leaving. "You're the best," he told her.

"At what I do, yes," Theresa replied softly. She doubted that her former protégé heard as he hurried from her office.

* * *

"You'll never guess who came to see me today," Maizie Sommers told her two best friends as they all gathered around the card table in her family room for their weekly game of poker.

"Considering all the traffic that your office sees, my guess would be just about anybody," Cilia Parnell quipped.

"Try harder," Maizie coaxed, displaying her customary patience. "Who's the one person you'd never think would come to see me? I'll give you a hint—it's about our matchmaking hobby," she told her friends, her eyes shifting from Theresa to Cilia and then back again as she waited for one of them to make a guess.

"Well, that narrows it down to half the immediate world," Cilia quipped. And then she took a closer look at her friend. "You look like the cat that ate the proverbial canary. I suggest you tell us or we'll be sitting here guessing all evening—and getting it wrong."

"Besides, I have to ask you something—and I have news," Theresa announced excitedly, "so get on with it, Maizie. You know I hate it when you just leave off the ending like that."

Maizie shook her head, surrendering. "Oh, all right. You two do take the fun out of this, you know that, don't you?" she said, feigning disappointment.

"The person's name?" Cilia prodded her friend, waiting.

She thought she'd at least get them to play along once or twice. However, since they didn't, Maizie told them, "Nikki."

Theresa looked slightly confused. "Your daughter, Nikki?"

"I've only got one daughter," Maizie pointed out, thinking it was needless to add her name in like that. "Yes. Nikki."

"She came to you about *matchmaking*?" Cilia asked, astonished.

"Yes," Maizie replied patiently.

It didn't make any sense to Theresa. "Well, your granddaughters are too young, so Nikki didn't come about them—" And then something else occurred to her. "How does she know that you're into matchmaking?"

To the best of Theresa's knowledge, none of their children knew anything about this side venture she and her two best friends were engaged in, despite the fact that they'd secretly arranged all four of their children's marriages.

"Apparently, Jewel told her," Maizie said, shifting her gaze toward Cilia.

Very little ruffled Cilia, but this clearly astonished her.

"*My* Jewel?" Cilia asked incredulously. This was the first she'd heard even a hint of this. Certainly Jewel had never said anything to her.

Maizie nodded. "*Your* Jewel," she confirmed. "But the really astonishing thing about this is that Nikki wants me to 'work my magic,' as she put it, to arrange a match for her friend Mikki. The two of them were roommates all through college and then they graduated medical school together—"

"Wait, so this Mikki you're talking about, she's a doctor?" Theresa asked, wanting to be absolutely sure she was getting the story straight before she allowed her imagination to run off with her.

"That's what usually happens when you graduate medical school," Maizie replied, her voice somewhat strained.

A doctor.

That was all Theresa needed to hear. She clapped her hands together in a sudden, uncharacteristically overwhelming burst of joy.

"Perfect!"

Maizie glared at her friend oddly, wondering what had come over her. "I think so, too. But why did you just say that?"

To explain, Theresa felt she had to backtrack a little. "Do you two remember Jeff Sabatino? That very handsome boy who used to work for me and then went on to open up his own restaurant right here in Bedford?" She looked at Maizie and Cilia, searching for any signs of recognition.

"Oh, that's right. Dinner for Two," Maizie recalled. "I went there when it first opened. Wonderful food. You taught him well," she told Theresa with a warm smile. And then she paused. "But why are you bringing him up?"

"Well, initially I wanted to ask if Nikki could recommend a good doctor for his mother. Seems Mrs. Sabatino refuses to go see one, and Jeff thinks she's in failing health," Theresa answered. "He asked me to ask you to ask Nikki—"

Cilia held up her hand, stopping her friend from continuing. "Cut to the bottom line, Theresa. None of us are as young as we used to be."

Maizie gave her friend a look. "Some of us are younger than others, Cilia—but yes, Theresa, what is the bottom line?"

Theresa told them Jeff's request. "Can you have Nikki recommend a good doctor—preferably female—with a good bedside manner?"

Maizie hadn't come this far in life without the aid of well-honed intuition. "There's more, isn't there?"

Theresa loved it when things just all seemed to come together. They all did.

"Well, Jeff is extremely good-looking. He's got chiseled features and liquid green eyes a woman could get lost in," she told her friends. "I'm speaking as a grandmother, by the way," she added in case her friends had any doubts about her interest in the young man, "and there's no girlfriend in the picture. He said something to the effect that he'd like to have kids, but he's too busy right now making a go of his restaurant—and taking care of his mother."

Maizie needed no more. Her eyes lit up. "We could get two birds with one stone."

"Exactly what I was just thinking when you started talking about Nikki's friend," Theresa said. And then a bubble-bursting thought suddenly occurred to her. "This friend, she's not a specialist, is she?"

"From what I remember, Mikki is an internist who specializes in cardiology," Maizie answered.

She smiled broadly at the two other women sitting at the card table. A single hand hadn't been dealt yet, and quite possibly, one wouldn't be, at least not tonight, Maizie thought. Tonight was for making plans and laying groundwork.

This was going to be good.

Maizie smiled broadly at her friends. "Ladies, I believe—in the words of Sir Arthur Conan Doyle's most famous character, Sherlock Holmes—that the game is afoot."

"I think the quote ran a little differently than that," Cilia corrected.

Theresa waved her hand at the possible contradiction. "The exact wording doesn't matter, Cilia. What does matter is that we just might have ourselves another match in the offing."

"Details," Maizie said aloud what they were all thinking. "Let's review details." She turned toward Theresa. "You tell us about your former protégé and then I'll tell you about my daughter's friend so that there are no surprises—other than pleasant ones, of course," she added.

Theresa rubbed her hands together and smiled broadly at the two other women at the table. "I *knew* today was going to be a good day."

"Put your cards away, Maizie," Cilia said, noticing that the deck was still out. "Looks like we've got work to do."

Chapter Two

"Oh, come *on*, Michelle. Come to the party with me. You work too hard, darling. Don't be afraid of having a little fun."

Mikki McKenna suppressed a deep sigh.

Served her right for answering her cell phone without looking at caller ID. But she'd just pulled into her parking spot in front of the medical building, and because of the hour, she had naturally assumed that it was someone in her office or the hospital calling.

Either that, or it was one of a handful of patients she'd entrusted with her private line in case of an emergency.

She hadn't expected her mother to call. That came under the heading of an entirely different sort of emergency. Something just short of the apocalypse.

It had been several months since she'd heard from

her mother. Thinking back, Mikki vaguely remembered that it had been right between her mother shedding Tim Wilson, husband number four, and going off on a cruise to some faraway island paradise, the name of which presently escaped her. Her mother *always* went off on a cruise after every divorce. Cruises were her mother's primary hunting grounds for potential new husbands. She kept going on different cruises until she found someone to her satisfaction.

"I'm not afraid of having fun, Mother," Mikki began, attempting to get her mother to see *her* side for a change even though, in her heart, it was a hopeless endeavor.

Veronica McKenna Sheridan Tolliver Wilson—her mother thought that having so many names made her seem like British royalty—immediately interjected, "Well, then come! This promises to be a really wonderful party, Michelle. Anderson throws absolutely the very best parties," she said with enthusiasm.

Anderson. So that was the new candidate's name. She wondered if the man had any idea what he was in for.

"I'm sure that he does, Mother," Mikki said, humoring her. "But—"

Veronica was quick to shut her daughter down. She'd had years of practice.

"Michelle, please, you need to have a little fun before you suddenly find that you're too old to enjoy yourself. Honestly, I don't know how I wound up raising such a stick in the mud," Veronica lamented dramatically.

Possibly because you didn't raise me at all, Mother, Mikki thought.

Between her parents' arguments and the almost-frenzied partying they both indulged in, singularly and together, she'd hardly ever seen her parents when they were still married.

She remembered being periodically dropped off to stay with various relatives as a child. As she got older, there were sleepovers at friends' homes instead, especially her best friend, Nicole. Envious of the family unity she witnessed, Mikki had made sure she was the perfect houseguest, going the extra mile by cleaning up after herself as well as her friend and even preparing breakfast whenever possible.

It was her way of ensuring that she would be invited back.

By the time she was twelve, her parents had divorced, and they'd professed to want shared custody of her—which meant, in reality, that neither parent really wanted to be saddled with her upbringing. Each kept sending her to the other. Money was substituted for love. The only interest from either one of her parents came by way of the actual interest her trust fund accrued.

If it hadn't been for her great-aunt Bethany, Mikki would have felt that she had no family at all. It was Great-Aunt Bethany who took an interest in her education and suggested that she consider attending medical school.

The latter had grown out of her having nursed an injured bird back to health after it had flown into the sliding glass patio door.

"You have a good heart and good instincts, Michelle. It would be a shame to let that go to waste," Great-Aunt Bethany had told her that summer, literally dropping a number of medical school pamphlets in her lap.

And that had been the beginning of Mikki's career in medicine. Her desire to help others, to make a difference, took root that summer. Very simply, it was the reason she had decided to become a doctor.

There had also been a small part of her—because for the most part, she had given up hoping to make any meaningful connection with her mother—that *did* hope her mother would be proud of her choice.

She supposed she should have known better.

"Well, if that's what you want, I suppose you should go for it," Veronica had said when she told her mother of her plans to go to medical school. "But personally, I can't see why you'd want to go poking around people's insides or whatever it is that you'll be doing. It's all so very icky, darling." Mikki could still picture the look of revulsion on her mother's face. "And you really don't have to do that, you know. You don't need to earn a living."

She let her mother go on trying to talk her out of her choice until Veronica lost interest in the subject.

Her mother was always losing interest in subjects, this included the various men that she had married. It was always "the next one" who promised to be better. Until he wasn't.

Watching her mother over the years, Mikki had become sure of one thing. That was *not* the kind of life she wanted.

"I'm only going to be in town for another day or two," her mother was saying now. "I don't know why you don't want to take the opportunity to come out of your shell and see me."

"Because I won't be seeing you," Mikki pointed out patiently. "Not personally, at least. You'll be partying with an entire ballroom full of people." Her mother was never happier than when she was the center of everyone's attention. And if she wasn't the center of attention, she did something to make that happen.

"And what do you want me to do, Michelle? Would you like me to sit by the fireplace like some old woman, mourning over things that didn't happen?" Veronica asked testily.

"No, Mother," Mikki replied. Because it was getting warm in her car, she put her key in the ignition and cracked open a window. She knew she could just as easily step outside, but she didn't want anyone overhearing her conversation with her mother. "I want you to do whatever makes you happy. Just like I want to do whatever makes *me* happy."

"But—"

She could hear her mother's frustration vibrating in the single word. But she'd learned not to allow her mother to play her.

"Sorry, Mother. That's my other line. I've got to go," Mikki told her, terminating the call.

Mikki held the cell phone against her for a moment and sighed. For once, there was no other incoming call, but she couldn't think of another way to get her mother to stop going on about the party at the Ambassador Hotel that she wanted her to attend. She had absolutely no use for those kind of vapid parties. Mingling with a roomful of strangers wearing overpriced clothes seemed like a colossal waste of precious time to her.

She supposed that the invitation could be her mother's way of trying to connect with her after all this time, but she really doubted it. Most likely, her mother was just trying to assuage her guilty conscience, although that in itself was rather unusual. Guilt and Veronica Mc-

Kenna Sheridan Tolliver Wilson did not coexist on the same plane.

Best guess was that Anderson Pierce, Veronica's boy toy of the month, had probably expressed an interest in meeting her daughter. Mikki wouldn't have agreed to go even if she *wasn't* busy, which she was.

All the time.

She had a thriving internal medicine practice associated with Bedford Memorial and, if that wasn't enough, she also volunteered on Saturdays at the free clinic.

She would sleep, she often said, when she was dead.

That would also be when she'd party, Mikki thought with a smile. When she was dead.

Her cell phone began to ring again. This time, she looked at caller ID before answering. The number on the screen was not familiar, but the name above it was.

She couldn't remember the last time she had spoken to Maizie Sommers.

"Mrs. Sommers?" she asked uncertainly, still not sure this was the woman she was thinking of.

The second the woman spoke, all doubt vanished. No one could pack as much warmth into a simple sentence as her best friend's mother could.

"Mikki, how wonderful to hear your voice again. How are you?"

"I'm well, thank you—"

"And busy, I hear," Maizie said, reading between the lines. "Nikki tells me that you're extremely busy these days."

"Well, yes, I am," Mikki admitted, but she didn't want to just brush the woman off because of that. She had some very affectionate memories associated with her best friend's mother. She'd lost count the number of times she had slept over Nikki's house—or the number of times she had wished that Nikki's mother was *her* mother, as well. "But never too busy for you, Mrs. Sommers. What can I do for you?" she asked, certain that the woman had to be calling about something. It wasn't like her to just call up for no reason.

"That's very sweet of you, Mikki," Maizie responded. "As a matter of fact, I did call you for a reason—"

Mikki was quick to tell the woman some necessary information. "I'm not in my office right now, but I know that my schedule is full for the next few days. However, I can see you either before office hours or after office hours, whichever would be more convenient for you, Mrs. Sommers."

She heard Nikki's mother chuckle softly. "You haven't changed a bit. You were always such a very thoughtful young woman. This isn't about me, dear. It's about—a friend," Maizie said, finally settling on a satisfactory wording for her request. "The poor dear hasn't been well lately."

Maizie paused for a moment to recall exactly what Theresa had told her. "She's been experiencing sharp pains in her abdomen and a general feeling of being unwell—"

"And what does her doctor say about her symptoms?" Mikki asked. She didn't like stepping on another doctor's toes unless she thought that there might be malpractice at the bottom of the case.

"That's just it, dear. She doesn't have a doctor. Absolutely refuses to go see one," Maizie added for good measure.

In this day and age, that didn't make much sense to her. "Why?" Mikki asked.

"It's a very sad story, really," Maizie said. "Her husband was misdiagnosed many years ago, and the poor man died as a result."

"And so now she doesn't trust doctors," Mikki concluded.

"No, not since that day," Maizie confirmed. "She's adamant about it."

"I can see why she might feel that way, Mrs. Sommers. But I can't exactly examine her against her will," Mikki pointed out.

Maizie started talking a little faster as she tried to change Mikki's mind about the matter. The way she saw it, there was a lot at stake here, more than just Jeff's mother's health.

"Her son is very worried about her," she stressed, continuing to set the stage. "If I can get him to bring her in to your office, can you give her a thorough examination?" Maizie asked. "You always had such a wonderful, calming manner about you."

Mikki laughed quietly. "I never examined you, Mrs. Sommers."

"I meant in general," Maizie said. "You know, I always thought you were the perfect friend for Nikki."

That brought back memories. "I always thought it was the other way around, really."

Mikki thought for a moment. Her cell was beeping, letting her know that this time there *was* another call coming in. However, she didn't want to put Maizie on hold or risk disconnecting. She wanted to finalize things before ending the call.

She thought for a second, then asked, "Could either you or your friend's son bring this lady to my office at eight tomorrow morning?"

"Eight?" Maizie repeated.

"I know it's early," Mikki allowed sympathetically. She was an early riser, but she knew a lot of people weren't. "But it's the only vacant time I have until the following day—"

"No, that's fine, really," Maizie assured her. "I was just making sure I heard you correctly." She knew Jeff's restaurant didn't open until eleven so, technically, he was free at that time in the morning. And from what Theresa had told her about the young man, even if he wasn't free, he would still make the appointment. "I'll have to call and make sure that he can bring her," she said, just so Mikki wouldn't suspect anything. "Is it all right if I call you back?"

"Of course it's all right," Mikki responded. "By the way, my office is in the medical building across the street from Bedford Memorial."

"I know," Maizie replied. "Just like Nikki's."

"Right." Mikki realized that of course Nikki's mother would be aware of that. Only her own mother had no idea where she practiced and what hospital she was associated with, Mikki thought ruefully. "Except that Nikki's office on the fifth floor. I'm on the third. Suite 310."

Maizie had already done her homework, but to keep from arousing Mikki's suspicions, she repeated, "Suite 310. Got it," Maizie said. "I really appreciate this, Mikki. Or should I say Dr. McKenna?"

"For you I'll always be Mikki," Mikki told the older woman.

"Yes," Maizie said warmly, "you will." And with all her heart, she sincerely hoped that this match, like the others so far, would work out. Very few young women deserved to be happy as much as Mikki did. "I can't tell you how much I appreciate this, Mikki."

"There's no need to thank me, Mrs. Sommers," Mikki told her with genuine sincerity. "I'm a doctor. This is what I do."

"You mean fit patients in at the last minute and come in to see them at hours that are way too early?" Maizie asked, amused. That wasn't a doctor, Maizie thought. That was a saint.

"Perfect description of my life," Mikki told her friend's mother with a laugh.

Memories from bygone days when her daughter and Mikki were just starting out on their journey came flooding back to Maizie. She found herself growing nostalgic.

"We really need to get together at your earliest convenience, dear."

"You're not feeling well, either?" Mikki asked, concerned.

"Oh, no, I'm fine," Maizie said quickly, not wanting her to get the wrong idea. "I just meant that I would love seeing you again. It's been a while, you know."

"Yes," Mikki agreed. "It has." And unlike her conversation with her mother a short while ago, Mikki found herself really wanting to get together with the woman on the other end of the call.

"Please call me the first moment you find time in that busy life of yours," Maizie encouraged.

"I'll be sure to do that. In the meantime, see if your friend can come in tomorrow morning. If he can't, call me back and I'll see what other arrangements I can make."

"I will," Maizie promised. "You were always one of the good ones, Mikki," she added.

"Funny, that was always what I thought about you, too," Mikki said before terminating the call.

The next second, her cell phone beeped again. "Dr. McKenna," she answered.

"I know who you are, dear." She closed her eyes. It was her mother again. "Have you had time to come to your senses about attending the party yet?"

"My senses are fine, Mother. And the answer is still no. Now, if you'll excuse me, I have a patient to see," she added quickly. "So goodbye again, Mother. Have fun at your party."

With that, she ended a call from her mother for a second time and hurried off to her office in order to officially begin her day.

Chapter Three

"I know you mean well, Jeffrey, but I don't want to go to see any doctor," Sophia Sabatino protested early the next morning.

The petite woman with salt-and-pepper hair was clearly in distress as she did her best to get her son to change his mind about "dragging" her off to some unknown doctor's office.

Like his two siblings, Jeff loved his mother dearly, and he usually gave in to the diminutive martinet, but not this time. He had made up his mind. This was too important. His mother needed to see a doctor, and he was taking her to see one before it was too late.

"Sorry, Mom," he told her. "I'm overriding you on this one."

She looked at him in exasperation. "You're taking

advantage of the fact that I'm too weak to put up a good fight," Sophia complained.

"Mom," he said patiently, "try to understand. It's *because* you're feeling so weak that I'm taking you to the doctor." Handing his mother her purse, he tried to get her ready to go with him.

Sophia defiantly dropped her purse to the floor. "I'm not going to see some quack and taking off all my clothes," she declared. Lifting her small chin, she crossed her arms before her chest.

"This isn't a quack—" Jeff began. This time, as he picked up the purse, he decided it was useless to return it to his mother. She'd only drop it again, so he slung the straps over his own shoulder.

"They're all quacks," Sophia informed him. "Your father, God rest his soul, thought all doctors walked on water, and look where it got him," she pointed out. "Dead," she declared when Jeff didn't answer her.

With determination, Jeff took hold of his five-foot-one mother's elbow and guided her out the front door. His goal was to get her to his car, which was parked in the driveway, as close to the front door as possible.

"They're not all like that, Mother," he said patiently. Bringing her to the passenger side, he held the door open for her. When she remained standing where she was, he very gently "helped" usher her into the seat. She remained sitting there like a statue, so he wound up having to strap her in before closing the passenger door.

Rounding the front of his car, he got in on the driver's side as quickly as possible. Weak as she appeared to be, he wouldn't put it past his mother to bolt from the car.

As he buckled up, then started the engine, his mother

picked up the conversation as if there had been no long pause.

"Of course they're all like that," she insisted. "It's all right, Jeffrey. Don't trouble yourself about me. I've had a long, full life. I'm ready to go meet your father."

"Well, you're just going to have to postpone that meeting, Mom," he told her firmly. "Tina, Robert and I aren't ready for you to lie down and die just yet."

"That is not your decision to make, Jeffrey," Sophia sniffed.

"It's not yours, either," he countered. "Lying down and dying isn't your style, Mom. You've still got years of nagging left to do."

Sophia opened her mouth to protest his disrespectful attitude, but instead of words, she uttered a surprised gasp as a hot wave of pain washed right over her.

Torn between thinking his mother was resorting to even more theatrics and believing that she really *was* in acute pain, Jeff drove faster.

"Hang on, Mom," he told her in the most calming voice he could summon. "It's going to be all right. My old boss's best friend's daughter recommended this doctor," he said, hoping that would give his mother some confidence.

Sophia's breathing was labored, but she still managed to ask sarcastically, "Couldn't find one on Doctors Are Us?"

It was more of a gasp than a question, and Jeff had to listen intently to make out what she was saying. He didn't want her dismissing the doctor he was bringing her to before she even met her. "Mom, I'm serious. *This* is serious—"

"I know." Pressing her hand against her abdomen,

Sophia closed her eyes. "Which is why I just want to be left alone to die in peace, not have some wet-behind-the-ears would-be doctor try to earn back his entire medical school tuition by treating me and pretending he knows what he'd doing."

"Mom—" Jeff's voice grew sterner despite his concern about her condition "—you're beginning to make no sense." His mother grabbed his arm. Her long, thin fingers felt surprisingly strong as she clutched at him. "Mom?" Concerned, he spared her a glance as he made a right at the corner. The hospital and the adjacent medical building were just up ahead.

Jeff didn't have to look closely to see the perspiration not just on his mother's brow, but on the rest of her face, as well. She had to be reacting to the pain she was experiencing, because it wasn't that warm a morning.

He'd waited way too long to strong-arm his mother. He just hoped it wasn't too late.

"Hang in there, Mom, we're almost there." He did his best to sound encouraging.

Clutching the armrest on her right and her son's arm on her left, Sophia waited for the pain either to pass or totally consume her. Her breathing was growing more labored.

"Do you think your father'll recognize me? It's been a long time and I'm not the young woman I was when we lost him," she said hoarsely in between panting.

"He won't have to recognize you, because you're not dying, Mom."

Parking in the closest spot available, which because of the hour was right up in front of the medical building, Jeff got out and quickly hurried over to the passenger side. Opening the door, he slowly eased his mother out and to her feet.

She looked rather unstable.

"Do you want me to carry you?" he offered.

"No." Sophia pushed his hands away. "I'm going to walk into this charlatan's office on my own two feet," she announced with far more bravado than she was actually feeling.

He knew it was an act, but for once he encouraged it. "That's my girl."

She looked at him accusingly. "If you really cared about me, you would have let me stay home and—" Her eyes widened as a sudden new onslaught of pain seized her, causing her to clutch at her abdomen. "Oh, Jeff, it hurts. It really, really hurts," she cried, all but sagging to her knees.

Jeff was torn between putting his mother back in the car and driving over to the hospital's emergency entrance and taking her upstairs to see the doctor who was waiting for her. The doctor who Theresa Manetti had assured him would be able to calm his mother down and find out what was wrong with her.

Jeff quickly weighed the options. He knew his mother. She'd balk at the emergency room, but he had managed to half talk her into seeing this doctor.

He went with door number two.

"What…what…are you doing?" Sophia gasped as he closed his arms around her. "I'm too heavy…for… you," she protested.

Jeff had lifted his mother up into his arms and proceeded to carry her into the medical building. "I've carried bags of rice heavier than you," he informed her, heading over to the elevator bank.

Because it was so early, there was an elevator car standing on the ground floor with its doors wide-open. It was empty.

He walked right in.

"Can you press three, Mom?" he asked, taking nothing for granted.

He could see more perspiration forming on her brow. She had to be in pain, he thought.

"This…is…a waste of…time," Sophia told him, trying hard not to gasp between each word. With visible effort as well as a show of reluctance, she weakly raised her hand and pressed the number three.

The doors barely closed before they opened again on the third floor.

Getting out, Jeff glanced at the signs on the wall, saw the arrow, then went right. Reading the numbers, he looked for suite 310.

Arriving in front of the door, he tried to angle the door latch with his elbow to push it down. When it didn't give, he tried again.

When the latch still didn't move, he used his elbow to bang on the door, hoping there was someone inside who would hear him and let them in.

Mikki had arrived at her office even earlier than she normally did. She'd let herself in through the back door because Angela, her receptionist, and the two nurses who worked for her, Virginia and Molly, weren't due in until regular hours, which officially began at nine.

Just because she was doing a favor for Maizie Sommers didn't mean that her staff had to be inconvenienced and come in earlier than usual, as well, Mikki thought. They worked hard enough as it was.

Mikki had just slipped on her white lab coat over a simple gray pencil skirt and blue-gray blouse when she heard a loud thud against the front office door.

Actually three thuds, she amended. Someone with a very heavy hand was either knocking on the door or trying to break it down.

Since she didn't keep a weapon in the office, she slipped her cell phone into her lab coat pocket after first pressing nine and one. All she had to do was press one more digit and the police would be on their way, she thought confidently. Bedford had next to no crime to speak of, and the well-trained police force, from what she'd heard, were eager to exercise their muscles.

Hopefully they wouldn't have to, she thought as she carefully approached her front office door.

"Who's there?" she called out.

"Dr. McKenna?" a deep male voice asked. "I'm Jeff Sabatino. I've brought my mother in to see you."

Relieved, Mikki quickly unlocked the main door—she hadn't had a chance to entirely open up the office yet.

She was about to say as much when she saw that the man she was speaking to was carrying an older woman in his arms.

"What happened?" Mikki asked, immediately opening the door wider and stepping aside to allow him to walk in.

"My mother started complaining of this stabbing pain on our way over here, and then when she got out of the car, her legs suddenly seemed to give way and she collapsed."

"I didn't collapse," Sophia protested indignantly. "I had a twinge of weakness. But I'm all right now," his mother declared with determination. "My son exaggerates things. I just want to go home and get into bed." She said the latter as if she was issuing an order to her son.

"Soon, Mrs. Sabatino," Mikki promised. "But I'd like to examine you first, if you don't mind."

"I do mind," Sophia retorted stubbornly.

"She's very grateful," Jeff corrected. His mother still in his arms, he looked around the general area. "Do you have an exam room?" he asked, then mentally upbraided himself. He hadn't meant to ask her that, he'd meant to ask where her exam room *was*.

Mikki smiled. "Actually, I do. I find they come in very handy in my line of work. Right this way," she told Jeff, leading him to the back of the office.

There were three exam rooms located in the back, one right next to the other. She opened the door to the first room and gestured for him to bring his mother into it.

"If you just have her lie down on the exam table," Mikki instructed, "I can get started."

Jeff did as she asked, placing his mother gently on the paper-covered examination table. Mikki couldn't help noticing that he had a very sensitive manner about him. It seemed almost in direct contradiction to the masculinity the tall, dark-haired man exuded.

"I've got her insurance cards and her driver's license," Jeff said, reaching for his mother's purse in order to produce the items.

But Mikki shook her head. "Don't worry about that right now. My receptionist isn't in yet. She handles all that. Right now, I'm more interested in why your mother had to be carried in—other than the fact that she didn't want to come to see me. Mrs. Sommers told me that you don't have any confidence in doctors," Mikki said, turning to her patient.

"I don't trust them," Sophia all but growled, keeping her hand firmly pressed against her lower right abdomen and grimacing.

"Mom!" Jeff admonished. He knew his mother had a take-charge attitude and she had no problem with making her opinion known, but he'd never seen her acting rude before, and it surprised him. It also wasn't any way to behave toward a woman who had gone out of her way to come in early and see her before office hours.

Mikki raised her hand, silently asking him to hold his peace for a moment. She was interested in her patient's response.

"Why not?" she asked the woman.

"Because a doctor killed my husband," Sophia cried with a hitch in her voice.

"Killed him or didn't save him in time?" Mikki asked diplomatically.

"What does it matter?" Sophia snapped. "He's gone. My Antonio's gone," the woman lamented.

"It matters," Mikki said gently. She began to slowly move her fingers along the perimeter of what seemed to be the painful region. "But right now, what matters more is what's going on with you. What are you feeling, Mrs. Sabatino?"

"Like someone's cutting up my insides with a burning-hot band saw." Her statement was punctuated with another audible cry of pain as she clutched at her abdomen again, almost pulling herself into the fetal position.

"I'm going to press a little more on your abdomen, Mrs. Sabatino. I want you to tell me if it hurts," Mikki requested.

"It hurts, it hurts," Sophia cried immediately.

"Mom, she hasn't touched you yet," Jeff pointed out, then turned toward the woman examining his mother. "I'm really sorry, Doctor," he began.

Mikki shook her head, wanting to put him at ease. "Don't be. Your mother's pain is very real," she told him. "She's obviously hurting without my touching her." As she spoke, Mikki subtly placed her hand first near his mother and then very gently on the area where she thought the pain originated.

She was right.

"Argh!" Sophia cried, her eyes narrowing as she angrily looked at the doctor. "You're *hurting* me!"

"I'm sorry," Mikki apologized. "I just want to be sure what's going on. How long have you had this pain?"

Sophia shrugged carelessly, avoiding her son's eyes as she mumbled, "A few weeks, I guess."

"Mom!" He'd only become aware of the problem in the last couple of days. "A few weeks? Why didn't you call me?"

Still avoiding his eyes, Sophia sighed. "I didn't want to bother you. You have that restaurant and everything. You're always so busy," she said just before her expression changed as she noticeably braced herself for another wave of pain.

Instead of reaching for a thermometer, Mikki opted to test her theory the old-fashioned way. She lightly placed her fingertips against the woman's forehead, finding it quite warm.

"Okay," Mikki murmured to herself. "I think that proves it."

"What is it?" Jeff asked, looking at the doctor quizzically. "Can you tell what's wrong with my mother?"

Mikki didn't want to be premature, but she had a very strong suspicion about what was going on. "Well, I think that we'd better get your mother into the hospital," she began.

"No, no hospital!" Sophia interrupted.

"Mom, let the doctor talk," Jeff told her, trying to get his mother to calm down long enough to hear the diagnosis.

"I don't care what she's going to say, I'm not going to die in a hospital," Sophia declared.

"No," Mikki responded with confidence. "You're not. But in order for you *not* to die, we need to get you there in time."

"In time for what?" Sophia demanded. "To cut me up into pieces?"

"No, just one piece," Mikki answered quite seriously.

"What is it, Doctor?" Jeff asked. His mother was clutching his hand and he wanted to do his best to calm her, but right now, he wasn't feeling all that calm himself. "What's wrong with my mother?"

"I need to run some tests," Mikki prefaced.

"I got all that. I understand. Just tell me what you *suspect* is wrong," Jeff said.

"Well," Mikki began, "with any luck—"

"Luck? You call feeling like someone set your insides on fire lucky?" Sophia cried indignantly. "Take me home, Jeff!"

"Let her talk, Mom," Jeff ordered, surprising his mother with his abrupt tone. He turned toward Mikki. "Doctor?"

"Best guess," Mikki said, enunciating every word

as she looked at the all but terrified woman on her examination table, "is that it looks as if your mother has appendicitis."

Chapter Four

The pain had momentarily abated, and Sophia sniffed. "Some doctor. She doesn't know what she's talking about," she told her son.

Jeff prided himself on his patience. He had a nearly infinite amount, both at work and when it came to dealing with his mother when she was being difficult. But his ample supply was just about used up this particular morning.

A warning note entered his voice. "Mother—"

Ignoring him, Sophia said, "I had my appendix removed when I was six," just before she suddenly doubled up in pain again.

"Are you sure?" Mikki questioned. "Forgive me," she quickly interjected, "but according to what you just said, you *were* six, and maybe you're not remembering things quite clearly."

"Of course I'm sure," Sophia bit off, annoyed that this slip of a girl was doubting her. "My mother told me that's what happened." About to continue, she suddenly grew very pale as she grabbed her son's hand. "I can't take this anymore, Jeffrey. Put me out of my misery."

Interceding, Mikki laid a gentling hand on the woman's arm to get her attention. "I fully intend to, Mrs. Sabatino, but not the way you mean." Mikki looked at Jeff. "I have to get her to the hospital and run some tests," she explained. "I still think it's appendicitis, but if it is something else, the CT scan and abdominal ultrasound should show us what we're up against."

Jeff looked at her, puzzled. "How can it be appendicitis if hers was removed?"

"She could be mistaken," Mikki pointed out. "At six, it's easy to misunderstand what's happening. Checking to make sure the appendix was removed is a simple process."

Sophia's laugh was harsh. "She just wants to get me into the hospital and do all those expensive tests on me."

He was aware that the doctor was doing him a favor, seeing his mother so quickly. She certainly didn't deserve to be treated this way. "I'm sorry about this," he apologized to Mikki.

Mikki's smile wasn't strained. Instead, it was understanding.

"It's okay, really," she told him. "I'm not offended. Your mother's afraid. Who wouldn't be?" she asked, giving Sophia an encouraging look. Sophia appeared to be totally oblivious to it. "Let me just leave a note for my receptionist and I'll ride over to the hospital with you and your mother," Mikki told him, picking up a pad and pen.

Jeff realized what a huge imposition this had to be for the doctor, especially since his mother wasn't even one of her regular patients. He could see why Dr. McKenna had been recommended to him. She seemed to have an infinite amount of patience.

"I really appreciate this, Dr. McKenna," he told her, then lowered his voice before adding, "My mother can be very difficult."

Mikki thought it prudent not to comment on that as she quickly wrote a note to her receptionist. He could say anything he wanted to about Sophia, but after all, the woman *was* his mother. If she agreed with his assessment, in all likelihood he would become defensive and that would make further communication difficult.

Being vague about her new patient's disposition was the best way to go.

"Let's just try to get her better," Mikki responded. "I'm going to call ahead so that we can get her into the radiology lab for those scans quickly."

With that, Mikki turned away in order to make her call.

The pain abated again for a moment. Concerned that she was disrupting his life, Sophia looked up at her son. "Just leave me here, Jeffrey. You have to get to work," she reminded him.

"Not for a few hours yet," Jeff corrected, "and anyway, I have people to cover for me. Let's just focus on finally getting to the bottom of this pain you've been having."

A ragged sigh escaped Sophia's lips. "Everyone dies, Jeffrey."

His mother could never be accused of being happy-go-lucky, Jeff thought. Or an optimist. "But not today," he told her firmly.

Sophia began to protest just as the woman she viewed as far too young to be a doctor, much less one who was exceptionally skillful, rejoined them.

"Everything's set," Mikki announced. "Let's get your mother over to the hospital. We'll use your car."

He didn't ask her why, but once they arrived in the hospital parking lot, the answer quickly became apparent. The doctor pointed out a space marked Physician Parking Only and told him to park there.

"My car's a small two-door," she explained, "and I wanted your mother to be comfortable." Quickly getting out of his vehicle, she told Jeff, "Wait here. I'm going in to get a gurney for your mother."

The moment the doctor walked in through the electronic doors labeled ER Entrance, Sophia grabbed her son's arm again. "I don't know about this, Jeffrey."

"Well, I do, Mom. We're here and we're getting to the bottom of all this. You almost cut off my circulation the last time you grabbed my hand."

"I won't squeeze your hand again, I promise," Sophia told him.

"That's not the point, Mom," Jeff said. "You're in a great deal of pain, and we need to find out why before your condition gets any worse."

"It's just indigestion," Sophia cried, trying not to writhe in pain. She was desperate to have him take her back home. She hadn't been inside a hospital since she'd lost her husband, and just being outside one brought back terrible memories.

"Enough excuses, Mom. You're having these tests and that's that," he told her firmly just as Mikki returned with a nurse and an orderly in tow. The latter two were pushing a gurney between them.

"Your chariot's here, Mrs. Sabatino," Mikki announced, smiling as she and the two hospital staff members approached Sophia.

Sheer panic entered Sophia's eyes when she looked up at her son. "Jeffrey?"

He forced himself to ignore his mother's pleading tone. "You're going in for those tests, Mom, and I'm going to be right there with you," he promised.

"Well, maybe during the ultrasound, but not during the CT scan," Mikki told him. Seeing the panicked expression on his mother's face, she added, "But I can come into the room with you."

That did little to comfort Sophia. "But I don't know you," she protested.

"Well, we'll use the time to get to know each other," Mikki told her.

Sophia murmured something under her breath that neither the doctor nor Jeff could make out. Jeff expected to see Mikki become annoyed. After all, she was bending over backward for his mother, who was being far from her usual genial self.

But the doctor only smiled, saying something encouraging to her in response.

Theresa had been right, Jeff thought as he accompanied his mother and her new doctor into the emergency room. Dr. McKenna was an absolute treasure. She was going out of her way to humor his mother and she hadn't lost her temper once. Most people did when his mother behaved this way. It wasn't often, but it was grating when it happened. He dearly loved the woman, but he wasn't blind to her faults.

Once inside the emergency room, his mother was taken to a curtained-off bed in order to prepare her for the CT scan, ultrasound and several other necessary tests. Jeff waited outside the curtained area as one of the nurses went in to help his mother change into a hospital gown.

"I'll take good care of her," Mikki said, coming up behind him.

Surprised—he'd assumed that the doctor had left for the time being—Jeff turned around to look at the petite dark blonde.

"What about your other patients?" he asked. He remembered that Theresa had told him the doctor had a full schedule today. That was why she'd asked him to bring his mother in so early.

"I take good care of them, too," Mikki answered with a smile.

He had no doubt that she did. There was something exceptionally competent about the woman. "I hope they're not all like my mother."

She laughed, and he liked the way her blue eyes crinkled.

"Oh, you'd be surprised," she told him. "A great many of my patients require a lot of hand-holding and reassuring."

"How do you do it?" he marveled.

"One hand at a time" was her answer.

Just then the nurse stepped out from between the curtained-off section. "She's all ready," the nurse told Mikki.

The latter nodded in response. "Then let's get the show on the road."

"Before you get started, Doctor," Jeff said, stopping her for a moment, "I just want to say thank you."

Her smile was warm and genuine. "No problem," Mikki said.

"But there will be," he replied with a sigh.

Mikki merely laughed in response.

The tests went far more quickly than he'd thought they would. He and his mother had arrived at the hospital at eight thirty. By ten fifteen the doctor had returned to tell him that she had all the results and she'd been able to diagnose his mother's condition.

When she paused for a moment, he immediately asked, "Is it appendicitis?"

"In a way," Mikki replied.

Anxiety sent a cold shiver down his spine. "There's more?"

"Yes." She chose her words carefully in order to explain the situation to him and not cause any undue confusion. "Fortunately for her, your mother's appendix apparently wasn't removed when she was six."

That didn't sound right at all to him, Jeff thought. Did the doctor have a macabre sense of humor? "What do you mean, fortunately?"

"Well, if your mother's appendix hadn't been there," she told him, "then we might not have ever known about the existence of the tumor until it was too late to do anything about it."

"Tumor?" he asked. It was all beginning to sound frighteningly surreal to him. "There's a tumor?"

She nodded. "It appears to be benign, but we won't know until we do a biopsy on it." She went on to paint a picture for him. "If the appendix hadn't been there, the tumor might have continued growing until it just burst on its own. The appendix got in its way, and the tumor was pressing on it. That's what caused your mother all that pain. We're going to be removing all of it, the tumor and her appendix."

He struggled to come to grips with the idea—and its possible implication. "Will this affect her in any way?" he asked.

"You mean the operation? Yes. Once it's over, the pain'll be gone," she told him. And then she smiled. "Your mother will be up on her feet and back to her old self in six weeks—or less."

That sounded almost as impossible as his mother having a tumor. "Really?" he questioned.

"Really," she assured him. "The whole thing sounds worse than it is, trust me."

He found himself doing just that. Which raised another question. "Who's going to be doing the surgery?" Jeff asked.

"Well, unless you have someone in mind who you want me to contact," Mikki began, waiting. When he didn't say anything, she went on to say, "It'll be me."

"Oh, I want you," Jeff told her with feeling. Then realizing how that had to sound, he tried to correct the impression. "I mean—"

Mikki laughed, and he caught himself thinking that the sound was almost endearing.

"I know what you mean, Mr. Sabatino, and I appreciate the vote of trust," she told him. Mikki glanced at her watch. "This is going to take a couple of hours once we get her ready and wheel her into the OR. After that, she'll be in recovery for another hour. From there, she'll be taken up to her room.

"If she responds like everyone else, your mother will be in and out of consciousness for the rest of the day, so I suggest that if you want to go to work, you do so without any guilt. Your mother's not going to be fully awake until sometime tomorrow morning, if not later."

"Is my mother still conscious now?" Jeff asked.

Mikki nodded. "We haven't given her anything to sedate her yet. So if you want to say a few encouraging words to her before we put her under, now would be the time to do it. They're getting the OR ready for her."

He heard something else in the woman's voice besides a recitation of the chain of events. "Then it *is* urgent," he asked her.

She didn't want to frighten him unnecessarily, but she didn't want to be evasive, either. Mikki offered him a smile. "Let's just say—without being melodramatic—that you brought your mother in just in time."

He was both relieved and stunned by the news. "Does she know?"

"I believe in keeping my patients informed, but not in scaring them," she replied. "Now, if you'll excuse me, I have to call my office to tell them I won't be in for a while—and then I have some less than fashionable blue scrubs to put on." She turned to go, but paused for a moment. She sensed that the tall, handsome man standing in the corridor needed a little reassuring. "She's going to be fine, Mr. Sabatino."

"Jeff," he corrected as he took in a steadying breath, thinking of the bullet they'd just been dodged. "Call me Jeff."

Mikki nodded. "Okay. Are you planning on staying here until your mother's in recovery—Jeff?"

He knew he wouldn't be able to focus if he went anywhere right now. "Yes, I am."

"Then I'll send someone out to let you know how it's going," Mikki promised.

"That's very kind of you," he told her.

"Practical," she corrected. "Otherwise, your imagination might just run away with you and then I might have another patient on my hands."

The moment the doctor left, Jeff went in to see his mother.

"Jeffrey, she's operating on me," Sophia lamented the second she saw him.

"I know that, Mom," he said kindly.

She looked somewhat surprised—and perhaps even upset. "And you're all right with this?"

"I wouldn't have it any other way, Mom," Jeff told her.

Sophia fixed the drooping shoulder of her hospital gown and drew herself up. "I think we need a second opinion."

"This from the woman who didn't want any opinion," Jeff remarked. He took her hand in his. Hers was icy to the touch. "Mom, you're just stalling. You know that a second opinion is most likely going to be the same as the one you just received."

"Maybe not," she cried.

It had never occurred to him until just now how much his mother looked like a little girl. A frightened little girl.

Closing his hand over hers, he assured her, "It's going to be fine, Mom. When you wake up, the pain'll be gone."

"Ha! You've obviously never had an operation," his mother said.

Jeff inclined his head, giving his mother her due. "Okay, let me rephrase that. The pain that brought you here will be gone."

Sophia snorted dismissively. "Trading in one pain for another doesn't exactly put me ahead of the game, you know."

"It does if the first pain can eventually kill you," he pointed out. The nurse entered just then, saving him. "They're going to get you ready for surgery now, Mom." He saw the clear panic in her gray eyes. "I'm going to be right here, waiting for you. I'll see you when this is all over," he promised.

"You hope," Sophia said.

"I know," he corrected. "Now, behave yourself," he told her, giving her hand a squeeze.

"Sir, we have to begin," the nurse gently prodded.

Releasing his mother's hand, he stepped back, about to leave.

"Tell Tina and Robert I love them," his mother suddenly said.

"You'll tell them yourself after this is over," he told her patiently.

"And if this doesn't turn out well, tell them that I forgave you," she called after him.

Jeff suppressed a sigh. "I'll tell them, Mom."

Chapter Five

Jeff felt antsy enough to want to set up camp right outside the operating room doors.

Since that wasn't really possible without having someone from security come to remove him, he settled on the nearby lounge.

Initially.

He really had intended on waiting there until his mother's operation was over. But despite his calm outward demeanor, when it came to being concerned about someone in his family, Jeff's patience tended to wither.

As a compromise, he settled for pacing in the lounge—and then up and down the corridor—slowly, doing his best to kill time and to get the antsy feeling under control.

For as long as Jeff could remember, his mother had been the family rock, the one everyone else turned to when they needed support. She wasn't supposed to be the one who needed support, but well, here they were.

Damn, but he hoped he'd done the right thing, bringing her to this doctor. He had a great deal of faith in Theresa Manetti, and in a roundabout fashion, Theresa had recommended this doctor.

But the doctor who had inadvertently misdiagnosed his father's condition had been recommended by a friend of his father's, and that had certainly turned out badly.

What if, well-meaning though she seemed, this doctor wound up botching the surgery she was about to perform on his mother?

He just couldn't seem to shake the sinking feeling that was snaking its way through him, undermining his confidence.

When his cell phone began to vibrate, he all but yanked it out of his pocket, fearing the worst. All he needed now was an emergency at work. He felt that he'd left the restaurant in capable hands, but there was always a chance that something unforeseeable would happen.

Jeff debated not answering his phone, just turning the cell off and slipping it back into his pocket. But the next moment, he acknowledged that was being cowardly. It wasn't the way he handled things or shouldered responsibilities.

Making himself look at the cell phone screen, he recognized the caller ID. Relieved and somewhat puzzled, he accepted the call.

"Theresa?" he asked.

"Hello, Jeff," he heard his former boss say. "I hope you don't mind my calling you."

"No, of course not." He just thought it rather odd—
Theresa wasn't in the habit of calling him to chat. "Is
there anything I can do for you?" he asked.

"No," she answered. Maybe it was his imagination,
but Theresa sounded rather uncomfortable. "Actually,
I'm just calling to see how everything went with your
mother's appointment with that doctor I told you about."

Jeff glanced over toward the OR doors. He'd seen
several hospital staff members go in after his mother
had been wheeled into the operating room, but there'd
been no one going in or out for the last forty minutes.
He told himself that was a good sign, but the truth was,
he didn't know.

"Well, I'm at the hospital," he answered rather guardedly. "My mother's being operated on right now."

He heard Theresa stifle a gasp. "My goodness. Jeff,
do you want me to come down there to wait with you?"
she asked.

The offer heartened him. Again, he couldn't help
thinking that Theresa Manetti was certainly like another mother to him.

"No, that's okay. There's no need for you to come. It
shouldn't be that much longer." Unless he thought of it
in seconds, because time was passing as if it was being
dragged by an arthritic turtle with a pronounced limp.

"You're sure?" Theresa didn't sound convinced.

"I'm sure," he told her with as much conviction as
he could muster under the circumstances.

"What kind of an operation is it?" Theresa asked.

"It's kind of involved," he admitted. At the moment,
he really didn't want to get into it, or explain the details.
"But the doctor seems confident that my mother's going
to be all right." He sighed, looking back at the OR doors

again. And then he shared what had been weighing on his mind. "The doctor said we got her here just in time."

"That's all your doing, dear," Theresa assured him. "If I remember correctly, you once told me that your mother can be a very stubborn woman."

"Well, yes, she is," Jeff admitted, although right now he didn't want to say anything that sounded the least bit negative about his mother.

He felt somewhat disloyal for having voiced that opinion. After all, he knew that she was only trying her best. It hadn't been easy for her, raising three kids as a single mother.

Theresa laughed softly. Then, as if reading his mind, she assured him, "All the best mothers are stubborn. Nothing wrong with that. Let me know how it goes, dear. Please call me if there's anything I can do."

"I will," he promised, "And thanks for calling."

"My pleasure, dear. Remember, call me," Theresa repeated just before she ended the call.

Sighing, Jeff tucked the cell phone back into his pocket.

There were a dozen things he needed to see to and a whole host of arrangements he had promised other people that he'd get to at his restaurant. He had a more than able crew at Dinner for Two, but it was up to him to keep everything running smoothly.

However, it felt as if everything had ground to a halt the moment he watched his mother being wheeled into the operating room. He really wasn't up to focusing his attention on anything else.

Parents were supposed to live forever. At least the good ones were, he thought as the corners of his mouth quirked in a smile. But his father had died all those years ago, and now his mother might be in danger of joining him.

No, damn it, he wasn't going to think like that. He'd gotten her here in time and Dr. McKenna seemed like she was very capable, so he was just going to stop entertaining these negative thoughts, stop feeling as if he was on the cusp of becoming an orphan and concentrate on the fact that his mother was going to make it through this operation and get well.

Jeff slipped his hand into his pocket and curled it around his phone. Contact with the phone made him debate calling his brother and sister to tell them what was going on. They were a close family, and he knew they wouldn't take kindly to being kept in the dark.

But what good would it do to make them worry? Robert was at a business meeting in Los Angeles today, and Tina had small kids. She couldn't rush over to the hospital with them, and finding a sitter would take a while. By the time either one of his siblings could get here, their mother would be out of surgery and most likely out of recovery, as well.

He'd rather be the bearer of good news than to be the one to lay worry on their doorsteps.

Out of the corner of his eye, Jeff saw one of the operating room doors open, and he was instantly alert. He held his breath as a nurse wearing scrubs and a surgical mask approached him.

"Are you Mr. Sabatino?" the nurse asked, peering up at him.

If he were any tenser, Jeff thought he'd probably snap in half. Automatically, he braced himself for bad news. "Yes, I am."

"Dr. McKenna sent me out to tell you that everything

is going according to schedule and that your mother is doing well. The operation's going to take about another hour, and the doctor suggested that you might want to get some coffee from the cafeteria downstairs. She said to tell you that the coffee from the vending machines up here'll kill you." The woman's eyes crinkled above her mask as she smiled.

Jeff almost laughed out loud at the comment. Tension began to drain out of him.

"Tell the doctor thank you," he said, "but I'll take my chances. I'm staying right here until she's finished operating on my mother."

The nurse nodded, giving no indication that his answer surprised her.

"I'll let her know." Her eyes crinkled slightly again above the surgical mask and she turned to walk back into the operating room.

He felt like a marathon runner who had just passed the halfway point.

He knew he should sit down, that marching up and down the length of the corridor was annoying to anyone who might be looking out of the doors located along the path he was taking, but he was just too restless to remain still for more than a couple of minutes at a time.

Finally, after what felt like forever plus twenty minutes, as he turned on his heel to retrace his steps past the OR doors for what seemed like the thousandth time, he saw them opening. This time, it was the doctor who came out.

Technically, because of the surgical mask, it could have been anyone in those blue scrubs, but he knew it was Dr. McKenna.

No one else had clear-water eyes quite that shade of blue.

Jeff cut the distance between them in less time than it took to think about it.

"Is the operation over?" he asked, suddenly afraid to ask the real question that had been preying on his mind for the last two hours.

"Yes," Mikki replied as she removed her mask. "And your mother, I'm happy to say, came through it with flying colors."

"Was it a tumor?" he asked, bracing himself for the worst while praying for the best.

"Yes, it was," Mikki replied. "But the preliminary biopsy said it was benign."

"Not malignant?" he asked, wanting to be very, very sure.

Mikki smiled. "Not malignant."

The dam gates opened and Jeff felt relief flooding through him. Overjoyed, he wasn't completely aware of what he did next. Wasn't aware of throwing his arms around the woman who had come bearing good news until he suddenly realized he was doing it.

He felt her blue-clad body against his as he spun her around in a circle.

The very next second, common sense made a belated appearance, and he quickly set her down again.

"I'm sorry, I didn't mean to—"

What he meant to tell Mikki was that he hadn't meant to get so personal, or so exuberant because he was afraid he'd insulted her.

Mikki absolved him of any guilt before he could get the words out.

"That's all right. That spin was probably the most

fun I've had in a month," she told him with a laugh.
Gaining her bearings, Mikki went on to say, "As I told
you earlier, your mother's going to be in recovery for
an hour, then they'll take her up to her room. You're
free to go visit her then, but she's probably going to be
asleep for most of that time."

He remembered her telling him that before and nodded. But he was more interested in something else she'd
said.

"When I asked you about the tumor, you mentioned
the word *preliminary*," he began, wanting to have everything spelled out for him. It was important that he
didn't misunderstand or get his facts mixed up.

By the expression on her face, he could tell that the
doctor knew what he was thinking. "We always like to
double-check results to make sure we haven't missed
anything, but right now, it's all looking very good, Mr.
Sabatino."

"Jeff," he reminded her.

"Right. Jeff," she repeated with a smile, just happy
that she was able to give the man good news.

For now he had just one more question. "And was
my mother mistaken about her appendix having been
removed years ago? I mean, it didn't grow back or anything, right?" he asked. "Just curious," he added, not
wanting her to think that he was in any way doubting
this woman who, in his opinion, had done the impossible and gotten his mother into the operating room.

"No, it didn't grow back, and yes, your mother was
mistaken about it being removed when she was a little
girl. As I said to you before we took her into the OR,
your mother's very lucky that she hadn't had her ap-

pendix removed the way she thought she did. Having her appendix there was what saved her life."

But Jeff shook his head. "*You* saved her life," he corrected.

She was definitely not going to argue with him. The operation had been a complicated one, and she was tired. Tired with a full day still ahead of her.

"Let's compromise and call it a team effort," she told him. "Now, I've got a whole office full of patients waiting for me," she said, already backing away. "But I will be back to look in on your mother tonight. And, of course, she'll have nurses monitoring her progress all day.

"If you have the time now," she said, raising her voice so that it would carry as she continued backing away, "stop by inpatient registration and give them your mother's insurance cards and her personal information. They get very nervous if that's not entered into the system for someone staying in one of the hospital's single-care units."

He had brought all the necessary papers with him. They were in his wallet.

"I'll do that," he told her. Then looking around, he asked, "Um, which way—"

"Inpatient registration is to your left," Mikki called out. Then, seeing him start to go the wrong way, she prompted, "Your *other* left."

He gave her a quick salute as he changed directions.

There was a lot of background noise, but he still managed to hear her laugh. The sound connected with something within him and buoyed him up.

Jeff hurried off to comply with the doctor's request.

After everything Dr. McKenna had just done, he wasn't about to drop the ball and neglect to register his mother.

He knew that they couldn't very well evict her—did patients get evicted from hospital rooms? he wondered. But he had no doubt that there was probably someone who was in charge of all this who might take it upon themselves to admonish Dr. McKenna about her unregistered patient.

After everything that she had just done, he wanted the doctor canonized, not given grief for an oversight, especially if it was *his* oversight.

And after he got his mother all squared away and properly registered, Jeff told himself, he was finally going to call Tina and Robert to let them know that their mother was in the hospital and that she had gotten through her operation with flying colors.

He intended to emphasize that she was doing just fine thanks to a very able, very kindhearted surgeon who also happened to be extremely sexy.

Maybe he'd keep that last part to himself, Jeff amended. At least for the time being.

Chapter Six

"Wow, you look as if you were rode hard and put away wet," Virginia Masson, Mikki's head nurse, commented the moment she saw her walking in through the rear entrance to the medical office.

"Words every woman longs to hear," Mikki said with a sigh.

The moment she'd finished the operation, she'd raced back into the locker room and changed out of her scrubs into what she'd worn when she came in this morning. She hadn't even bothered look in the mirror before hurrying back to the medical building—on foot because she'd made the trip to the hospital in Jeff's car.

Mikki ran her fingers through her hair in lieu of using a brush and looked in the general direction of the waiting room. "How many are out there?" she asked.

"Enough to put a chill in your heart if you were Marie Antoinette," Virginia answered.

In other words, a crowd scene, Mikki thought. "My, you are colorful today. Fill me in on why after I see a few of these patients."

"They all waited for you, you know. Angela did her best to try to get them to reschedule, but they wanted to wait it out." Virginia shook her head. "Must be wonderful to have so many adoring fans," the dark-haired nurse teased.

"They just appreciate a good doctor," Molly Campbell, her other nurse said, coming out of the last exam room to join them.

Mikki flashed the second nurse a smile as she shrugged into her lab coat. "You—I think I'll keep," she quipped. "Her—I'm not so sure about," she added, nodding toward Virginia. "Okay, who's in exam room one?" she asked, mentally rolling up her sleeves to plunge into her day.

"Emily Rodriguez. She's waiting to hear the results of the lab tests she had done last week." As Virginia spoke, she produced several sheets of paper the lab had sent over and placed them in the file Mikki had just picked up from the reception desk.

A quick study, Mikki scanned all three sheets before she reached exam room one. She looked over her shoulder at the remaining files on the desk.

"Maybe I should have gone home," she murmured to herself.

Centering, she summoned a wide smile, opened the door to the exam room and walked in. "Afternoon, Emily. Sorry to keep you waiting so long—"

It was nonstop from there. Mikki saw one patient

after another, pausing only to take an occasional sip of coffee, which went from hot to lukewarm to cold. She hardly noticed. All she cared about was that it was black. As such it served as her fuel and kept her going.

By three forty-five, she had made a sufficient dent in her patient load. Going nonstop, she'd almost managed to catch up.

Tired, Virginia leaned against the wall as another patient received her paperwork from Angela and left the office. The woman looked at Mikki, not bothering to hide her admiration.

"Damn, lady, you have to let me know what brand of vitamins you're on, because they just can't be anything normal people have access to," Virginia commented.

"It's called fear of letting anyone down," Mikki told her.

Overhearing her, Molly laughed. "Like you ever could," the young redhead responded.

Mikki nodded toward the waiting room. "How's it going out there?" she asked.

Virginia looked down at the sign-in sheet. "Eight more patients and then I believe freedom is yours," she said, peering out into the waiting room to double-check. And then she looked again. "Oh, wait, I think we have a walk-in."

Mikki closed her eyes. "I don't know if I'm up to this." Her day had felt like an endless parade of patients. "Angela, see if Dr. Graves is available to take the overflow."

"No," Virginia told her, forestalling any such inquiry. "I think you're going to want to take this one yourself."

Mikki was about to tell her head nurse that the woman was crediting her with being superhuman. But just as she opened her mouth to protest, she caught a glimpse of the person who had just entered the waiting room—a deliveryman holding a large crystal vase filled with what looked like at least two dozen long-stemmed pink roses.

Virginia looked at her in utter stunned surprise and cried, "You're seeing someone and you didn't tell us?"

It took a second for the words to sink in. Another to realize that both nurses *and* the receptionist were staring at her. Virginia appeared a little envious, while Molly seemed almost hurt.

"No, I'm not seeing anyone," Mikki responded. "There must be some mistake." Leaning over the reception desk to peer into the waiting room, she told the deliveryman, "You have the wrong suite."

The young man looked at the clipboard tucked under his arm, then at the card attached to the arrangement. The name on the envelope was facing him. He raised very pale eyebrows to look at her. "You Dr. McKenna?"

"Yes, but—"

"Then I've got the right suite. I need one of you to sign for this," he said, setting the vase down on the reception desk and holding out his clipboard.

Both nurses were now flanking Mikki. "If I sign for them, do I get to keep the flowers?" Virginia asked her.

Molly, a veteran of fifteen years of married life, made a dismissive noise. "I'd probably have to die before Walter would send me flowers that looked like that," she commented. "Hell, I'd probably have to die before he sent me a single daisy."

"They certainly are beautiful," one of Mikki's remaining patients said from the waiting room.

Well, there was no denying that, Mikki silently admitted.

Quickly signing her name on the line the deliveryman pointed out, she returned the clipboard to him. Pausing only to take the small envelope that had come with the flowers and pocketing it, she turned toward her receptionist and said, "Please send in the next patient, Angela."

Virginia looked at her, totally mystified. "Don't you want to know who the flowers are from?" she asked Mikki as she went into exam room three to prepare it for the next patient.

"They're probably from some broker who's trying to sell me a retirement plan," Mikki guessed. "This is just a sales ploy, and things like this pop up all the time. I'll look at the card later."

There was no one in her life who would be inclined to send her flowers, much less do it. And there certainly was no occasion, large or small, coming up in the near future that necessitated any sort of celebration. She was convinced that it had to be some mix-up at the florist, and she'd see about straightening it out after she saw her last four patients of the day.

And once she did that, she still had to get back to the hospital, Mikki reminded herself. She wanted to look in on Mrs. Sabatino before she called it a day. Mikki was fairly confident that the woman would still be asleep— and would remain that way through the night—but that didn't change the fact that she wanted to check on her just to see how her impromptu patient was doing.

"Okay, you did it. Mr. Meyers was your last patient of the day," Virginia announced three hours later.

Crossing the reception area, the head nurse locked the office door, then turned around to waylay her friend and employer before Mikki had a chance to slip away.

"*Now* will you look at that card and see who sent you those flowers?" she asked.

Mikki suppressed a laugh, not wanting to hurt the nurse's feelings. "I think you're more excited about those flowers than I am," she told Virginia.

Frowning, Virginia shook her head. "That's another thing. You're *not* excited about them. What's wrong with you?" She waved her hand in the general direction of the vase with its profusion of pink roses. "These are gorgeous, not to mention expensive. If someone had gone to all this trouble for me, *I'd* certainly be excited." She looked at Mikki closely. "*Do* you know who sent them?" she asked.

"No," Mikki admitted. And then she let the woman in on a little secret. "And as long as I don't know, I can pretend that they *are* for me. Once I look at the card and see that the florist did make some kind of a mistake, then I'll know that they're not for me."

Virginia read between the lines. "Then you *would* like to get flowers," she concluded, happy to discover that Mikki was as normal as any other woman.

"I'm not a robot, Virginia. Of *course* I'd like to get flowers. But I'm pretty confident that these aren't for me, so—"

Uttering a sigh of exasperation, Virginia reached into Mikki's lab coat pocket and, with the expertise of a pickpocket, pulled out the card.

She was taller than Mikki and held the envelope out of the doctor's range while she extracted the card from the envelope.

"Give that to me, Virginia," Mikki ordered.

But it was too late. Virginia had managed to read the card. She looked at Mikki, curiosity etched on her brow. "Who's Jeff Sabatino?"

The name immediately caught Angela's attention. "Isn't that the name of the woman you operated on this morning?" she asked.

Mikki had called her receptionist from the hospital just before she began the operation. She gave her the woman's name and asked her to make an entry in the ongoing schedule that she kept on her computer.

Pulling the lanky nurse's arm down to secure the card from her, Mikki scanned it herself—twice to make sure she hadn't made a mistake.

"'Thank you for everything. Jeff Sabatino.'" The last time Mikki read the card out loud.

"Yes," she said slowly, remembering to answer Angela's question. Saying nothing further, Mikki tucked the card back into her pocket. And then she looked at the roses as if seeing them with fresh eyes. Despite her resolve to appear nonchalant and unfazed, she felt a smile slip over her lips.

The flowers really *were* absolutely beautiful, Mikki thought.

The next moment she realized that three sets of eyes were unabashedly watching her as the three women all grinned.

Mikki turned to her employees. They seemed to have questions sizzling on their tongues, all but bursting to come out. That was when she realized that what had been written in the card might have sounded a little ambiguous, causing her staff to start thinking all sorts of things.

That was all she needed.

"Not a word," Mikki warned. Shedding her lab coat, she left it slung over the back of Angela's chair and picked up her purse where she'd left it in the desk drawer. "I'm going to the hospital to see how my patient is doing. After you lock up, you can all go home," she told them. It was an order, not a suggestion. "You've put in a longer day than usual," she said, letting herself out into the hallway.

"You, too, apparently," Virginia called after her.

Mikki didn't have to turn around to know that the woman was grinning.

She took her car this time, parking it in the spot reserved for her.

Getting out, Mikki quickly hurried into the hospital and then up to the sixth floor, where most of her patients usually went after surgery.

She tried not to think about the flowers or the card that came with it.

Or the man who had sent them.

Consequently, she couldn't think of anything else, not just because the roses were so beautiful, but because no one had ever sent her roses before. She'd had grateful patients before as well as grateful family members, but none of them had ever sent her flowers.

The truth was, Mikki wasn't really sure how to react, or what she was supposed to say. She knew she had to acknowledge receiving the flowers. But there was this unusually warm feeling rattling around inside her that she wasn't exactly sure what to do about.

This isn't about you. It's about your patient, remember? Think about your patient. That's why you're here.

Check in on her, then check out. Her son is probably long gone, back to his home or his restaurant.

The thought that the man worked in a restaurant reminded her that she had been running on empty all day.

You haven't eaten since this morning, Mikki. Get something to eat. You need fuel.

As soon as she finished with Mrs. Sabatino, she promised herself.

Mikki paused at the nurses' station when she got to the sixth floor. It was her habit to always check in with the head nurse first.

"How's Mrs. Sabatino doing?" she asked the nurse who was watching the monitors.

The nurse, an older woman who had been on the job for close to twenty-five years, seemed a little preoccupied and didn't respond at first. However, when Mikki asked about Mrs. Sabatino again, the nurse suddenly jumped, as if she was being caught falling down on the job. She flushed.

"What? Oh, Mrs. Sabatino is fine. Doing fine," the nurse corrected herself. Glancing at notations on the computer that had been left by the last nurse, she said, "She's been asleep this entire time."

"But you have been monitoring her vitals, right?" Mikki asked. "And checking her temperature every hour?"

The nurse nodded. "Every chance I got."

Mikki thought that was rather an odd way to word the response, but it was getting late and it was obviously the end of this nurse's shift. The woman's eyes appeared to be drooping. Maybe the woman was just overly tired, she reasoned.

No more than me, Mikki thought.

She was just going to look in on Mrs. Sabatino herself and then, since the nurse had nothing to report, she was going to go home and collapse, Mikki promised herself. She was hungry, but there was nothing in her refrigerator that could pass for edible food and she was far too tired to stop to pick up something on the way home.

She'd get something tomorrow on her way in, Mikki promised herself as she went down the hall. Missing a couple of meals wasn't going to kill her.

The door to room 616, Sophia Sabatino's room, wasn't closed. There wasn't anything unusual about that. Mikki knew that it was easier for nurses to go in and out this way without waking up the patient.

Slipping quietly inside the room, she could hear gentle snoring. Just as she'd expected, Mrs. Sabatino was asleep.

That was good, she thought. The longer the woman slept, the longer her body would have to heal and recover from the trauma of surgery.

Moving in closer, she checked the monitors beside the woman's bed, all of which were hooked up to her patient, including an IV drip.

Turning to leave, Mikki didn't see him until he moved. Jeff Sabatino was sitting in a chair all the way over in the corner like a silent sentry, taking everything in.

Mikki dragged air into her lungs as she consciously stifled a gasp. Doing her best to collect herself, she said, "I didn't realize that you were still here."

Jeff smiled at her, rising. "I didn't mean to scare you," he apologized. "You said you were going to look in on her. So I thought it was only fair, since you were going out of your way like this for my mother, that I'd stay here and wait for you."

"That really wasn't necessary," she told him, aware that he had to be exhausted. He probably wasn't accustomed to running on empty the way she was. "If I had anything to tell you regarding your mother's condition or her operation, I'd call you."

Jeff nodded. "I know that, but I just thought that my being here was more personal—since you were going the extra mile the way you did this morning," he reminded her. "Besides, in my present state of preoccupation, if I went into work, I might wind up poisoning one of my patrons."

"I guess that wouldn't exactly be a selling feature for your restaurant." Without realizing it, she caught herself laughing.

Jeff nodded. "See? You agree. Everybody's better off with me here." An ironic smile curved his lips. "This is my first day off in five years."

Another workaholic, like her, Mikki thought. She glanced over toward her patient, who was sleeping soundly. "Well, then I'm glad it ended well," she told him.

"Yeah, me too," he replied with genuine sincerity.

Jeff was looking at her, rather than his mother, as he said it.

Chapter Seven

Jeff nodded toward his mother. "Do you really think she's going to sleep through the night?" he asked Mikki.

"I'd count on it," Mikki told him. "Feel free to make the most of what's left of your first day off in five years," she encouraged, smiling.

He looked back at his mother. "I feel like I'm too drained to do anything but go to bed and sleep myself," he confessed.

Mikki laughed. "I hear that," she agreed. She felt exactly the same way. It had been a tough day for both of them.

Just then, her stomach rumbled loudly, embarrassing her.

It was impossible to ignore, so she owned up to it. "Sorry," Mikki murmured, flushing. "It likes to complain."

"Have you had dinner yet?" he asked her.

"Dinner?" Mikki echoed with a laugh. "I haven't had lunch yet."

When she went nonstop the way she had today, eating was not only pushed to the back burner, it didn't really register with her at all. Not until she realized just how hungry she really was.

"Hey, my restaurant's not too far from here," he told Mikki. "The least I can do is feed you." Jeff felt responsible for her hunger, cornering her the way he had early this morning, and he wanted to make amends.

But Mikki shook her head. "Thank you, but I like to be conscious when I'm eating so I can enjoy the food, and right now, I'm *really* tired," she emphasized. "I need to get myself home before I wind up falling asleep behind the wheel."

What she said raised another concern for him. "If you're that tired, I could drive you home," he offered. Then, thinking that she might feel he was coming on too strong, Jeff amended his offer. "Or I could pay for a cab to take you home. I don't want anything happening to you on my conscience."

Mikki waved away his offer as well as his guilt. "There's really no need, thank you. And just so you know," she added with a smile, "I've been taking care of myself for a very long time. I can get home from here in my sleep—but I promise I'll stay awake for the trip," she added, amused. "Now go enjoy the rest of your day off, Mr. Sabatino."

"I'm trying to," he answered, looking at her pointedly.

But because he didn't want to make the doctor nervous, he made no further offer, allowing Mikki to leave first.

She'd just reached the room's threshold when she remembered. Pausing to look over her shoulder at Jeff, she said, "By the way, thank you for the roses. They're beautiful, but you really didn't have to go out of your way like that."

Oh, good, he thought, she'd gotten them. He was beginning to think they hadn't been delivered when she hadn't said anything.

"Neither did you," he countered.

She knew that arguing the point with him was only going to be a waste of time, so instead Mikki inclined her head and murmured, "Touché," just before she left the room.

Mikki could feel herself smiling during the short trip to her house.

Because she wanted to be able to get to the hospital as quickly as possible whenever she was needed, Mikki had deliberately purchased a house in a development close to Bedford Memorial.

Consequently, she really could drive home in her sleep the way she'd joked, although she had never attempted to put that to any sort of a test—and never would.

Twelve minutes after she had left Sophia Sabatino's room—and the woman's handsome son standing in it—she was crossing the threshold to her tastefully decorated, modest little two-story house.

That was when she remembered that she had left the vase with its plump pink roses back in her office. The roses would have looked nice on her coffee table. But then, she told herself, seeing them gave her something to look forward to when she went in tomorrow morning.

Not that she didn't look forward to seeing her patients, she quickly amended as she made her way up the stairs to her bedroom. She really did like interacting with the people who sought her out, hoping that she could fix what was wrong with them.

That was the wording her very first patient had used when the woman had come to see her. The woman had asked her to "fix what's wrong with me." Mikki recalled the phrase often and fondly.

As a doctor, she liked to think of herself in that capacity, as a person who fixed people. That was her real purpose in life.

She might have been oversimplifying it—or maybe even elevating it—but she knew that at least for now, that was how Jeff Sabatino viewed what she'd done. She'd fixed his mother.

Reaching her bedroom, Mikki stepped out of her shoes, quickly shed her clothes and threw on a short, well-worn nightgown.

Before going to bed, she usually undertook a nightly ritual which involved brushing her hair and her teeth and moisturizing everything that she didn't want to become wrinkled over time. But tonight, she really did feel too exhausted to lift a brush or patiently slather cream on various parts of her body.

She got as far as sitting down on her bed, contemplating just what she could actually do before she totally ran out of steam. That was when she realized that her eyes had shut and she'd slumped over onto the bed. With effort, she tried to give herself a pep talk to sit up and at least get into bed properly.

But all she managed to do was to pull her pillow far-
ther under her head.

She didn't remember anything else.

Not until she felt her watch rhythmically pulsing
against her wrist.

Never one for trinkets and toys, much less jewelry,
Mikki had indulged herself in getting a watch that could
be linked up with her smartphone. That way she'd never
miss a call because she was unsuccessfully hunting for
her phone, something she had a habit of misplacing
more often than she cared to admit.

Because she hated being late for anything, Mikki
had her watch set to go off in the morning, waking her
well in time to get ready for work.

Blinking now, she focused in on her watch. As her
brain cleared, she noticed that she had slept straight
through the night, something that was highly unusual
for her.

"I guess I really was tired," Mikki murmured to herself as she got up and hurried into the bathroom to take
one of her six-minute showers.

It was something she'd perfected during her intern-
ship after graduating medical school. She didn't feel
human until she had her morning shower, but time was
so precious, she'd endeavored to take shorter and shorter
showers until she'd learned how to do everything she
needed to, including washing her hair, in six minutes
flat.

Mikki could get dressed even faster, putting on only
a smattering of makeup before going downstairs.

Reaching the kitchen, she remembered that she had
yet to go to the supermarket to replenish her empty
pantry or her refrigerator. Currently, there wasn't any-

thing in either one that could be used in preparing the simplest of meals.

Mikki sighed.

Ordinarily she didn't frequent fast-food places or drive-throughs, but necessity was what caused a great many things to happen. At the very least, she needed coffee, and if she was stopping for that, she might as well get it from a place that offered something that could pass for breakfast on the run for those who were starving. And she was.

As Mikki got behind the wheel of her car, she thought of the offer Jeff Sabatino had made to her last night. Too bad the man's restaurant didn't open early for walk-ins, she silently lamented. She might have taken him up on his offer this morning. However, she'd heard that his was strictly an establishment that required reservations, so its not being open early was a moot point.

For the most part, she wasn't a reservations type of person. She was more of a spur-of-the-moment type, because she never knew when she'd actually have a moment to spare for anything beyond just seeing her patients.

So, resigned, Mikki forced herself to pull up to the first fast-breakfast place she passed on her way to Bedford Memorial. It was either that or putting up with hunger pangs.

Rather than idling in the drive-through line, spewing exhaust fumes as she waited to pay for a meal she really wasn't looking forward to consuming, Mikki parked her car as close to the front entrance as she could, then hurried into the establishment.

The line inside to order was far shorter than what was snaking its way around the building outside. Placing her order, she took the empty paper container that the sleepy-eyed teenager behind the counter handed her and went to get her coffee.

She'd just finished filling the container and securing the lid when she heard the teenager call out her number.

Efficiency always made her smile, and she smiled at the barely-out-of-high-school teen who handed her the bagged breakfast she'd ordered.

Mikki glanced at her watch as she went out through the establishment's swinging doors. It had taken less than five minutes from the time she'd ordered to the time her meal was ready. Pretty good. She hoped she could say the same thing about the meal itself.

Beggars can't be choosers, Mikki reminded herself, starting up her car again. And while she hadn't begged for the meal but paid for it, she felt that the saying still applied in this case.

At least the aroma that began to fill her vehicle was promising.

Pulling into her reserved spot at the hospital, Mikki was tempted to take a few minutes to eat her breakfast before going up to see Mrs. Sabatino.

But she had long ago schooled herself to put responsibility ahead of any personal gratification, and that included having a meal. So breakfast would have to wait until she looked in on Mrs. Sabatino.

Barring some sort of unforeseen emergency, her visit wouldn't take long, Mikki promised herself.

Crossing her fingers, Mikki got on the elevator and pressed six.

As always, she stopped at the nurses' station first.

"How's my patient?" she asked the woman seated at the desk. When the older woman eyed her blankly,

Mikki gave the woman the particulars. "Sophia Sabatino, room 616. She was operated on yesterday morning."

"Oh, right, that one," the nurse said as if a light had suddenly gone on in her head. She checked notations on the computer before saying, "She woke up a few times during the night, according to the chart entries. Sara said she kept asking if she was dead."

As Mikki recalled, Sara was the night-shift nurse for this part of the floor.

When the nurse paused, Mikki nodded. "That's the one. Are Mrs. Sabatino's vitals steady?"

The nurse laughed. She didn't even have to check the numbers before she spoke. "Hell, we should all have vitals like that one. Except for her operation, from all indications that woman's as healthy as a horse."

"Sounds good," Mikki commented.

Although she was always prepared for them, she didn't really care for surprises. She preferred seeing nice, steady numbers that neither rose nor fell.

Thanking the nurse, Mikki made her way to her patient's room.

Because she had a feeling that the woman preferred ceremony, Mikki knocked lightly on the door frame before walking into Sophia Sabatino's room.

"How are you feeling today, Mrs. Sabatino?" Mikki asked the woman, trying to sound as cheerful as possible despite the frown she saw on the woman's lips.

Sophia groaned dramatically before answering. "Like I died."

Mikki had a feeling that she could easily be sucked into a whirlpool if she attempted to reason the woman out of the dramatic assessment.

Instead, she said, "Well, I'm happy to say that you didn't." She gave the woman a bright, heartening smile. "And we'd like to keep you that way."

"I was right, wasn't I?" Sophia challenged, her surprisingly dark eyebrows drawing together over the bridge of her nose.

"Right about what?" Mikki asked.

"That I don't have an appendix," Sophia answered a little impatiently.

"Not anymore, you don't," Mikki replied, choosing her words tactfully. She didn't want to get into any sort of a debate as to why Sophia's mother might have lied to a six-year-old about having her appendix removed. "I removed it during your surgery."

"So it *was* appendicitis?" Sophia asked, her face scrunching up in confusion and disbelief.

"Not exactly," she said, realizing that the woman had probably forgotten what she'd explained to her just prior to the surgery. "You had a sizable tumor that was pressing against your appendix. The tumor had actually wrapped itself around your appendix and one of your ovaries. We had to take that out, as well."

"My ovary?" To Mikki's surprise, the woman chuckled to herself. "Well, I certainly haven't had any need for that for a long time," Sophia confided. And then she looked up at her surgeon. "And that's it?" she asked, amazed. "That's all you found?"

"Most people would say that was quite enough," Mikki assured her. "It everything continues going the way it has, you should be feeling better very soon."

"I'm feeling better now," Sophia told her, contradicting the doctor's assessment.

Mikki smiled. "That's probably because you're still on pain medication."

Sophia looked at her, horrified. "You mean I'm getting drugs?"

"It's standard procedure, Mrs. Sabatino." She could almost see the wheels in the woman's head turning, and it wasn't hard to guess what she was thinking. "Don't worry, you won't get hooked on them. You're being given just enough for your weight and height to take the edge off your pain, nothing more."

"Well, I certainly hope not," Sophia said primly, smoothing out the covers on either side of her.

"Give the doctor a break, Mom. The woman undoubtedly saved your life."

Sophia's entire countenance changed as she looked over toward the doorway and saw her son walking in. She seemed to light up.

Her warm smile lasted for a moment, then faded a little as she looked behind him. She pretended to sniff. "Where are the others?"

"They'll be here, Mom," Jeff said patiently, obviously accustomed to his mother's abrupt shifts. "Their hours aren't as flexible as mine are." And then, his smile widening, he glanced toward the doctor. "Good morning, Dr. McKenna. I thought I'd find you here." Recalling their conversation from last night, he asked, "Have you had anything to eat yet?"

"No, not yet," she admitted. She saw that he was about to say something, most likely about her unintentional starvation diet, and she quickly added, "But soon. Soon," she repeated for emphasis. "I'm going to have breakfast as soon as I finish making my rounds and leave the hospital," she said pointedly, looking at her patient.

Chapter Eight

"Well, my offer still stands," Jeff told her the next moment. "Any time you'd like to drop by my restaurant to take me up on that dinner—or lunch—just give me a call and I'll make sure there's a table reserved for you."

"He really does cook well," Sophia chimed in, her voice still a little reedy. The woman's eyes crinkled at the corners as she smiled at Mikki. "I taught him everything I know," she added with more than a little pride.

Jeff smiled, humoring his mother. He refrained from contradicting her, because the truth of it was, his mother *had* taught him everything she knew. The problem was, his mother's culinary abilities could be judged to be utterly unremarkable and very basic at best.

Sophia Sabatino had taught him how to find his way around a kitchen because, as a widowed mother, on occasion she'd had to leave him in charge. More than a few times she'd been forced to work late or to cover for someone at the social services office. It had been left up to Jeff to feed his siblings something that went beyond junk food.

As with everything else he undertook in his life, Jeff went the extra mile. He didn't just make sure his siblings did their homework, he quizzed them to make sure the lessons they read sank in.

And he didn't just throw together whatever he found in the refrigerator and call it dinner—he would painstakingly hunt for recipes that would turn what he had to work with into something enjoyable to eat. He started out by following recipes he found on the backs of boxes of rice and spaghetti, then very soon he began to augment them, creating recipes of his own.

It wasn't long before he'd started making dinners for his mother. From there, he became a short-order cook at a local restaurant in order to earn some extra spending money. Working for Theresa's catering company had been a natural step for him to take. There he'd learned a great deal, which eventually led to him opening up his own place.

"You must be very proud of him," Mikki told Jeff's mother.

Looking at her now, Mikki was willing to bet that Sophia was prouder of her son than her mother ever was of her. She couldn't remember a single instance when Veronica had displayed anything that even resembled pride. Her mother hadn't attended her medical school graduation because it would have meant rescheduling a cruise with husband number three.

Sophia beamed as she looked in her son's direction. "I am at that," she said.

Mikki noted that her patient's countenance toward her had changed since yesterday. The initial belligerence tinged with antagonism Sophia had displayed had completely disappeared, as had the suspicion in her eyes when Sophia regarded her.

"So—" Mrs. Sabatino did her best to sit up "—when can I go home?"

Mikki had pulled up entries the night nurse had logged. "Soon," she answered after scanning them quickly.

"Today?" Sophia pressed eagerly, obviously no longer feeling the need to act reserved or be on her guard.

Mikki smiled at the older woman even though she was forced to shake her head.

"Not that soon, I'm afraid. But soon," she reiterated. Making a final notation on the chart, Mikki looked at her watch. Why weren't there more hours in a day and more minutes in an hour? "And now I have fifteen minutes to get to the office before my first patient starts complaining that I'm late."

Jeff had remained on the sidelines, watching this woman who seemed to him to be a perfect combination of grace and effortless competence. It struck him that the doctor was the closest thing to flawless he had ever encountered. Now that the danger was over, he found himself intrigued.

"What about breakfast?" he asked. How did she manage to run on pure energy the way she did if she didn't eat, he wondered.

"Oh, it's in the car," Mikki answered, suddenly remembering that it was still waiting for her. "I'll eat while I'm driving over to the medical building."

Because of the business he was in, he met a lot of

people who lived to eat. Apparently, his mother's surgeon was one of those people who ate to live—when she remembered to eat.

"That can't be good for your digestion," Jeff commented.

He was right, but Mikki didn't have time to get into any sort of a debate about that.

"Better than not eating at all," she countered with a smile. Turning toward her patient, she said, "I'll see you tonight, Mrs. Sabatino." Then, nodding at Jeff as she hurried out, she said, "Goodbye."

His mother made a clucking noise he'd become all too familiar with throughout his childhood. "If that young woman's not careful, she's going to wind up in her own hospital."

"That's just what I was thinking, Mom," Jeff agreed. Turning toward her, he gave his mother his full attention. "So, how are you feeling?" he asked. Then, his eyes meeting hers, he emphasized, "Really?"

"Achy, tired and these stitches are beginning to hurt," his mother answered. "But I feel a lot better than I did yesterday morning and the days before that," she confessed.

There was no way to adequately describe the relief he felt. Smiling warmly, he said, "See? Sometimes it pays to listen to your son."

"Don't let it go to your head," Sophia warned, then reminded him, "Even a broken clock has the right time twice a day."

He laughed. "Ah, there's the mother I know and love. Welcome back, Mom," he said, bending over to kiss her forehead. Now that he was no longer worried about his mother's health, things could get back to normal again.

"I've got to get to the restaurant today. There's a retirement party coming in at four."

"Go, go, I'll be all right," Sophia told him, wiggling her fingers in his direction in lieu of waving him off.

"Robert and Tina are coming by to see you today," he reminded his mother in case she'd forgotten. Ready to leave, he asked, "Can I bring you back anything?"

"You're coming back?" Sophia asked, pretending to be surprised. She wasn't fooling him. He knew that his mother clearly expected him to return to the hospital.

But he played along, knowing his mother liked reinforcement. "Of course I'm coming back, but it'll be around seven. Sam said he'd cover for me tonight, and he's capable enough," he told her before she could ask, mentioning his assistant manager. He really had to go, so he cut the exchange short. "What can I bring you?"

Sophia answered without any hesitation. "Grandchildren."

It was a familiar topic. Hearing her touch upon it heartened him, because that meant that she really *was* on the path to making a full recovery. These last few days, when he'd spoken to her on the phone, she hadn't said a word about future grandchildren.

"Tina and Robert have that department covered," Jeff told her.

"Those are *their* kids. I'm taking about your kids," Sophia emphasized.

Jeff paused to press another kiss to her forehead. "Welcome back, Mom. Gotta go."

"You can't run from this forever," she reminded her oldest child.

"I'm not running, Mom. I'm just taking care of business—just like you taught me to," he added for good measure.

He heard his mother sigh dramatically just as he reached the doorway. The woman should have been an actress, not a social worker. His mother truly had missed her calling, he thought fondly.

"See you tonight," he told his mother right before he left.

His mother meant well, he thought, taking the elevator to the ground floor. Undoubtedly, there was some handbook that urged all mothers to attempt to indoctrinate their offspring with a desire to produce short versions of their own kind. And he understood that, he really did.

He had nothing against kids, Jeff thought as he left the hospital. He actually liked kids, and he was crazy about his niece and nephew. They were at an age where they were messy, sticky and noisy, but he still regarded them all with a great deal of affection. But to produce a kid of his own would require a female participant. Someone he'd presumably date before anything of a more serious nature happened between them.

However, in the last couple of years, the restaurant had consumed all of his time. This thing with his mother had been an aberration. He normally didn't have this kind of time to spare. Since this had turned out to be a life-or-death scenario, he'd had to *find* the time. There was no other choice. He'd taken charge because neither his brother or his sister could get their mother to do anything she didn't want to, and the situation had been dire.

Life or death or *dire* were not words that came up in reference to dating someone, so the whole concept of dating *anyone* fell by the wayside. And if he wasn't dating someone, there was no way he could make his mother's heartfelt wish come true and present her with a grandchild.

Not unless he won one in a lottery.

Still, Jeff caught himself thinking as he drove to Dinner for Two, if he *were* inclined to date someone, he'd like whoever fate eventually sent to cross his path to look like that sexy blonde surgeon who had saved his mother's life.

Jeff had no doubt that Dr. Mikki McKenna was already taken. An intelligent, highly professional woman who looked as if the term *knockout* had been coined with her in mind *had* to be in a relationship. Granted, he hadn't noticed a ring on her left hand, but that didn't mean anything. She probably didn't wear a ring because rings could get caught on any number of things, and as a doctor, she couldn't risk something like that happening.

Pulling into his parking space, he blocked out all further thoughts of the doctor, his mother and the grandchildren he hadn't given her.

It was time to focus on work.

Happily, there were no crises for him to handle.

The retirement party went off without a hitch, as did the regular service. Mercifully, everything went smoothly.

So smoothly that he caught himself thinking about his mother's doctor on several occasions during the course of the day.

He found himself wondering if she was going to be there tonight. He intended to swing by the hospital to see his mother just as he had promised. That led him back to thinking about Mikki. He tried to remember just when she had turned up at the hospital last night to check on his mother.

What are you, twelve? Trying to get a glimpse of the hot girl at school? Jeff admonished himself. His thoughts should be centered on his mother and his restaurant, not on what time Dr. McKenna would be making her rounds at the hospital.

Still, if he had any questions about his mother's condition, it wouldn't be a bad thing to run into the doctor, now would it?

You're rationalizing and you know it. What's come over you? he silently demanded, annoyed with the way he was behaving.

As the day wore into evening, he decided that he wasn't doing any good here. That being the case, he might as well leave.

"Hey, Sam," he called out to his assistant manager, "I'm heading out."

Across the kitchen, Jeff's assistant manager nodded. "About time," he quipped. "Say hello to your mom for me. Tell her we're all rooting for her and wish her a speedy recovery. How long is she going to have to be in the hospital, anyway?"

That was still up in the air. He hoped to have an answer when he saw the doctor tonight. "My guess is at least another day."

Sam nodded, taking the information in. "Maybe Ginny and I will go see her tomorrow. We'll bring Wendy," he added, referring to his two-year-old daughter.

Great, Jeff thought. That would only encourage his mother to ramp up her crusade for more grandchildren.

Still, he appreciated the man's thoughtfulness. So out loud he said, "That'll be great. Kids always cheer my mother up."

"Then we'll definitely bring her," Sam promised, calling after his boss.

When he arrived at his mother's room, Jeff found her talking to the nurse on duty. Her doctor, however, was nowhere to be seen. He wondered if he'd missed her.

"Hi, Mom. Brought you your favorite," he said, placing the bag from his restaurant on her serving table. Rather than say anything, or look pleased by the offering, his mother just lay there. Because she hadn't made any response, Jeff just kept talking. "Chicken parmesan."

His mother appeared even more dismayed. "I can't have anything solid until tomorrow night," she finally lamented.

"Okay." He was nothing if not flexible. "I'll bring you a fresh serving tomorrow night."

"You don't have to get rid of it," Sophia told him, suddenly brightening right before his eyes. "Maybe Dr. McKenna would like to take it home with her for dinner."

That was when he realized that the doctor had walked in right behind him. Turning around, he flashed a smile at the blue-eyed, diminutive doctor. "Hi."

Mikki nodded in acknowledgment. Noting that she had obviously walked in on something, Mikki framed her question carefully, just in case the thing her patient was saying that she could take home was her son. "Take *what* home with me?"

Jeff was quick to come to her rescue. "My mother's

talking about the chicken parmesan that I brought her tonight."

Oh, dinner. Relief washed over her, quickly followed by her thinking that she couldn't get over how thoughtful Jeff Sabatino was when it came to his mother.

It reminded her just how empty her own upbringing had been. It had never occurred to either one of her parents—when they were still together—to do anything even remotely thoughtful for her or for their spouse. And once their divorce was final, the idea of maintaining any sort of family unity, much less behaving thoughtfully, never seemed to occur to either one of her parents.

Mikki reiterated what Sophia had already told her son. "I'm afraid your mother can't have anything solid to eat yet."

Sophia didn't hesitate speaking up. "I can't, but you can."

Mikki looked at her blankly. "Excuse me?"

"Why don't you take my serving of chicken parmesan home with you?" Sophia suggested. "It's a shame to let good food go to waste, don't you agree, Doctor?"

"Yes, of course," Mikki agreed. "But I don't think—"

"Then the matter's settled," Sophia declared, bringing her hands together in what passed for a commanding clap—at least until she got stronger. "Jeffrey, give the doctor the dinner that you brought for me."

Mikki tried to talk the woman out of giving away her dinner to her one last time. "Oh, no, Mrs. Sabatino, I couldn't just—"

"Of course you could," Sophia insisted. "This isn't a bribe. We're still going to pay your bill," she told the young doctor.

His mother was a master when it came to talking faster than anyone else could think. "Mom, stop railroading Dr. McKenna and let her talk," Jeff said. He turned toward Mikki and apologized. "She has a habit of talking right over a person, so you have to speak up for yourself or you're a goner."

"Jeffrey," Sophia protested. "You make me sound like a cartoon character."

"Not a cartoon," he amended. "But definitely a character," he said with affection. "But she does have the right idea," he continued, turning toward Mikki. "Why don't you take this home with you?" He held the bag out toward her.

"Don't you want it?" she asked him.

He grinned. "I have more than my fill, trust me. This way, maybe if you like it, you'll change your mind about having dinner at my restaurant."

"It's not that I don't want to have dinner at your restaurant—"

Jeff wasn't his mother's son for nothing. He'd picked up some things along the way, including seizing opportunities when they presented themselves. "Great, then how about Thursday night at eight o'clock?"

Mikki didn't see how she could gracefully turn him down again.

So she didn't.

Chapter Nine

Mikki's landline was ringing when she opened her front door and walked in.

The old saying about there being no rest for the weary flashed through her head. After locking the door behind her, she quickly crossed the living room to the phone. She was afraid the call might be from her mother, wanting to discuss the possibility of her attending yet another party, cruise or some other function that she had absolutely no interest in going to. However, since she knew that it could also be someone from the hospital or one of her patients, she couldn't very well ignore it.

The caller ID made her smile even as she released a long, exaggerated sigh. Pulling the phone over to her, she sank down on the sofa and picked up the receiver. And relaxed.

"Hi, stranger. Haven't heard from you for a while.

What's up?" And then Mikki sat up, alert, as she answered her own question. "Wait, don't tell me. You're pregnant."

"No," Nikki Sommers-Wingate replied with a laugh. "I'm not. Although I have to admit that Luke and I have been thinking about it. Three is such an uneven number," she laughed.

"Unless you have twins again," Mikki pointed out. "And then you're up to five."

"Well, it's nice to know that at least your math skills are still good," Nikki responded, "which is more than I can say for your phone etiquette."

Mikki had no idea what her best friend was talking about. But it was really nice to hear the sound of her voice no matter what she was saying. Too much time had passed since they last spoke at length. "Okay, what are you talking about?"

"As in using the phone," Nikki prodded.

"Sorry. Still lost," Mikki told her.

"As in you haven't called me since forever," Nikki spelled out for her. Ever since she'd asked her mother to step in and find someone for her best friend, Nikki had had to sit on her hands to keep from calling Mikki to find out if there was anything new in her life. But curiosity had finally gotten to her, which was why she was calling her friend now—and doing her best to make it sound as if this was nothing more than just a friendly call. "How are things going?"

"Fine," Mikki answered, refraining from saying anything about her newest patient—and her good-looking, attractive son. "And the phone works two ways, you know. You could call, too."

"I *am* calling," Nikki pointed out. "And I repeat, how are things?"

Mikki shifted slightly in her seat, wondering if her best friend had suddenly become a mind reader.

"Okay. Mother's been calling, trying to get me to come to one of her parties. She's in between husbands and I think she wants a morale boost from me, of all people."

"Your mother's always done very well without any boosting," Nikki mused.

Mikki laughed softly. "Amen to that." She put her feet up on the coffee table.

"Anything else new?" Nikki asked nonchalantly.

Dropping her feet to the floor again, Mikki sat up. *Did* her friend know about her possible dinner out? "Like what?"

Nikki had wanted her friend to volunteer the story on her own, but apparently that wasn't going to happen, so she prodded gently. "Oh, come on, Mik. Word has it that someone sent you half the long-stemmed pink roses in Bedford."

"Not half," Mikki protested, then reluctantly corrected, "Just two dozen."

"Close enough," Nikki granted, then got down to the important part. "So who sent them?"

Mikki shrugged, even though her friend couldn't see her. "Just this guy."

"Okay, so far, so good, but I need more," Nikki prodded. This was like pulling teeth. "What guy?"

"This restaurateur," Mikki finally said. She didn't want to make a big thing of it. She knew her friend wanted to see her find someone and if she said anything about Jeff, Nikki would have her married off before the end of dinner. "I agreed to see his mother before office hours. Turns out she had a tumor plus some other complications. I operated. He sent flowers, end of story," she said with finality.

"End of story?" Nikki questioned. "And he's a restaurateur?" Those details she'd already gotten from her mother. She wanted to get to the meat, to find out how Mikki felt about the man. "Didn't he at least offer to give you a free meal for saving his mother's life?"

"Well, yes, he did, but—" Mikki stopped abruptly. Something wasn't adding up. "Wait, how do you know I saved his mother's life?"

"I know you," Nikki reminded her, brazening it out. "You said 'complications.' I extrapolated."

"Uh-huh." Okay, maybe she bought that. But there was still something being left out. "And who told you about the flowers?"

Nikki merely laughed. "I have my sources. So when are you going?"

The question caught her off guard. "To what?"

"To the restaurant. C'mon, Mikki, keep up here," Nikki stressed, trying to get answers out of her friend without Mikki getting suspicious.

Mikki felt herself getting warm and she pushed the feeling away, doing her best to remain aloof from the situation. "He said he'd reserve a table for me at eight tomorrow."

Finally, they were getting somewhere, Nikki thought. "So what are you wearing?"

"Nothing—"

"You're going naked?" Nikki teased. "That's a daring move, but you do realize that there are laws about that, right?"

"Very funny," Mikki responded. "I said 'nothing' because I'm not going."

There were times when her best friend made her want to tear her hair out. It was time for her to stop hiding, step up and become part of life. "For heaven sakes, Mikki, why not?" she cried.

Mikki blew out a long breath. "Because."

"*Because* is a conjunction," Nikki pointed out patiently, "it's not a reason. A good-looking man wants to express his gratitude by springing for dinner at a place he owns. Why would you want to insult him by not going?"

"Who says he's good-looking?" Mikki asked, suspicion creeping into her voice again.

Nikki never missed a beat. "You did."

"No, I didn't," Mikki protested.

So she explained it to her—and hoped the explanation would be enough to deter Mikki's suspicions. "Again, I know you. If this was a man whose face would stop a clock, or who was a wizened old troll, you wouldn't hesitate taking him up on his invitation—after all, it's a public restaurant. But you're thinking of *not* taking him up on his invitation and there can only be one reason for that. Because he's good-looking and you're afraid it might lead to something."

Listening, Mikki could only shake her head. "You know, you're letting all this talent go to waste. You should have been a police detective or a private investigator."

"And with that fancy footwork of yours, you should have been a professional dancer," Nikki countered. Maybe this was going to work out after all. "Now, as your best friend, I'm telling you to take this man up on his offer and show up at his restaurant tomorrow."

Mikki was honest with her—there was no point in telling her friend that she was wrong or imagining things. "I don't want to risk starting anything."

Nikki fell back on a play on words. "I have news for you—you've been eating for a long time now."

Mikki sighed. "You know what I mean."

Nikki grew serious. "Yes, I do, and you can't keep running like this."

"I'm not running," Mikki protested with a touch of indignation she did her best to pull off.

"Sprinting, then," Nikki corrected. "Look, I know how you feel. You're afraid of getting involved with someone, but that fear is keeping you from possibly finding more happiness than you could imagine. I was afraid, too, once—"

"You had the normal kind of fear that everyone has."

"Right," Nikki agreed. "Just like you."

"No, not just like me," Mikki contradicted. "I have a family with a history of making colossal mistakes." Scenes from her mother's multiple marriages did a slide show through her brain, and she shuddered. "Soul-destroying mistakes."

"Mikki, you're not your mother," her friend insisted. "You're smarter, sharper and kinder—and that's just for openers. What you're experiencing, oh beloved friend of mine, are cold feet."

Mikki laughed harshly. "Try frozen."

"There's one good way to warm frozen feet up, you know," Nikki said.

Mikki sighed. "You're just not going to give me any

peace until I wind up going to this man's restaurant, are you?"

"Good call. I always said you were brilliant. I intend to hound you forever," Nikki answered. "Or at least until you go and have that dinner."

"Okay, okay," Mikki cried, surrendering. "I'll turn up at his restaurant tomorrow."

"Wonderful!" Nikki declared, victorious. "Dinner's at eight, right?"

"Right," Mikki answered uncertainly, wondering what her friend was up to.

"All right, I'll be at your place tomorrow at six."

Mikki nearly choked. "Why?"

"To help you get dressed," Nikki answered matter-of-factly.

Okay, she needed to set limits here. "Nik, you might not know it, but I've been getting dressed by myself for years now."

"Right," Nikki agreed. "And you look very competent and authoritative, but that's not how you want to look on a date."

This wasn't a date, it was dinner, Mikki silently protested. Out loud she said, "No offense, but I don't need supervision."

"I've known you since elementary school," Nikki reminded her. "And in that time, you've never gone out on a date."

"And I'm not going on a date now," she insisted. "I'm just having dinner. By myself," she emphasized. Before Nikki could say otherwise or embellish on the situation, she told her friend, "I'm going to the man's restaurant and he's going to be working."

"He told you that?" Nikki asked. This was not what

her mother was supposed to arrange, she thought, wondering if signals had gotten crossed.

"No," Mikki admitted, "but I'm going there during work hours…"

Nikki suppressed a guttural sound of frustration. "How is it that you're so brilliant and so totally naive at the same time?" she asked.

"I am *not* naive," Mikki retorted.

Nikki merely laughed. "Right. None are so blind as those who refused to see. I'll be there tomorrow at six. And don't bother coming up with any excuses or stories why you can't go. You're going if I have to strap you to the roof of my car and drive you over there myself."

When had Nikki gotten so bossy? "Are you this dictatorial with Luke? Because if you are, he has my condolences."

Nikki ended their conversation by telling her friend, "You're going," and then hanging up.

This was a bad idea.

Mikki was convinced of it.

The phrase kept whispering through her head each time she thought about tomorrow night or about possibly eating her dinner while seated across from Jeff. And each time it whispered through her mind, her stomach tied itself up into knots. Big, fat, hard knots.

Nikki was absolutely right. The thought of spending any time with someone as good-looking as Jeff Sabatino made her more nervous than she could put into words. *Not* because he was handsome, but because he was handsome *and* nice.

It was his personality and the fact that he was good

to his mother that made her so nervous. Because it was precisely that nice quality that attracted her to him.

Attraction was the first rung on the ladder that would eventually lead to disaster.

Mikki frowned, trying her best to ward off a meltdown.

Nikki was right in one respect. Mikki wasn't her mother. She wasn't shallow like Veronica, falling for looks and hoping that things would work out. Though she was willing to admit that looks could be very compelling, they were also only skin-deep, and while it was nice to have a handsome face to look at, that didn't complete the portrait.

It was the person beneath the looks who counted.

But the bottom line was that she didn't want to fall for a person's looks, for his decency or his personality. Because inevitably, one or all three would lead to a place called heartbreak.

She'd watched her mother fall apart and carry on too many times. There was no way she would ever emulate that behavior. No way would she ever be in her mother's one-size-too-small shoes.

She was still giving herself that pep talk the next day. Half a dozen times she had reached for the phone, ready to call Dinner for Two to cancel her reservation.

She made her last attempt to pick up the landline receiver as Nikki was fussing with her makeup. She had gotten as far as saying, "Hello, I have a reservation tonight for eight o'clock—"

She didn't get the opportunity to give her name because Nikki very deftly, without missing a beat, terminated the call.

"Yes, you do," she said when Mikki looked at her accusingly as she hung up the receiver. "And you are keeping that reservation come hell or high water, remember? I'm driving you."

Mikki caught a glimpse of herself in the mirror. Nikki had gone all out, she thought, trying not to smile at what she saw. "I can drive myself."

"I have my doubts about that," Nikki replied.

Mikki made another attempt to dissuade her. "You can't drive me, because then I'll have no way to get home."

Nikki paused just before putting finishing touches on her hairstyle. "Well, maybe Jeff can drive you home."

"No," Mikki replied firmly. She knew what her friend was thinking. She wanted Jeff to bring her home because she was hoping there would be a natural progression of things after that. Well, that wasn't going to happen.

"All right, how's this? We'll compromise," Nikki suggested. "You can drive yourself to the restaurant— but just to be sure that you do get there, I'm going to follow you in *my* car."

"Don't you have a life?" Mikki demanded.

"A very full one, thank you," Nikki replied. "And that's why I'm doing all this, because I'm hoping to help you get a life like mine, too. I want you to have what I have."

Mikki rolled her eyes. "I never knew you had this matchmaking streak in you."

Nikki neither admitted to nor denied the accusation. "Life is a series of evolutions," she simply informed her friend. "There," Nikki pronounced, standing back. And then she declared, "Perfect, even if I do say so myself.

And now, Cinderella," she said, glancing at her watch, "if you don't want to miss the ball, I suggest you hustle yourself into that chariot of yours before it suddenly turns into a pumpkin."

"If there's going to be any pumpkin-turning going on here, my money's all on you, kid," Mikki said.

"Okay, stop stalling, grab your purse and let's go."

Mikki looked at her incredulously. "You're really going to follow me there?"

"Every inch of the way."

Mikki took another stab at getting her friend to reconsider. "Isn't Luke going to be annoyed that you left him with the kids all this time?"

"Only if I tell him that I let you go to the restaurant alone," Nikki answered.

Mikki just shook her head. "You're both crazy, you know that?"

"That's why we go so well together," Nikki said with a grin. "He wants you to be happy, too. Now, let's go!"

Resigned, wanting to get this over with, Mikki picked up her purse. She could feel the giant butterflies already climbing on for the ride.

Chapter Ten

Mikki glanced in her rearview mirror every few minutes. And each time she did, her best friend's silver-gray sedan was right there behind her.

True to her word—or threat—Nikki followed her all the way to Dinner for Two. Not only that, but when she parked in the restaurant's lot, so did Nikki.

Expecting her friend to accompany her into the restaurant to make sure she went in, Mikki braced herself. Much as she loved Nikki, she was going to put her foot down and tell her she needed to get back into her car and go home to her husband and kids.

But she didn't have to.

Nikki remained in her vehicle, giving no sign that she was about to get out. The woman did, however, stay and watch her, obviously waiting for her to enter the restaurant.

Mikki had no doubts that the pediatrician would remain in the parking lot for at least several minutes to make sure that she didn't slip back out of the restaurant and make good her escape.

Putting her hand on the brass door handle, Mikki turned and, with a smile frozen in place, she waved at her best friend.

What's the matter with you? Go inside already. You're behaving like some paranoid lunatic. This is just dinner, not a betrothal. The man's grateful to you for saving his mother's life and he's just trying to show his gratitude. He's not about to whisk you off to a Las Vegas wedding chapel on his private jet. If you even mentioned that to him, he'd probably turn pale and run for the nearest exit—while calling to have you committed.

Take a deep breath and get in there, Michelle McKenna.

She braced her shoulders and, still giving herself a pep talk, she entered the restaurant. The interior looked like something out of a painting of an old English manor. It even had a fire going in the redbrick fireplace. The words *warm and cozy* sprang to mind.

A hostess standing behind a tall desk looked her way the moment the doors closed behind her. "May I help you?" the young woman asked.

"I think I have a reservation for eight," Mikki told her uncertainly. Jeff had told her that he would reserve a table for her, but for all she knew, he might have gotten busy and forgotten all about it.

Or maybe he'd just decided to think better of the situation and hadn't made the reservation at all.

The hostess smiled pleasantly and asked, "Name, please?"

"Dr. Michelle McKenna," Mikki told her.

She watched as the hostess scanned the computer screen, running her well-manicured, light pink–polished index finger along it a total of three times. Finally, the young woman looked up apologetically.

"I'm sorry. I'm afraid I don't see you on today's list. Could the reservation be under someone else's name?" she asked helpfully.

"No, it was just for a party of one," Mikki told the hostess. She *knew* she shouldn't have come. Embarrassed, all she wanted to do was to leave. "I'm sorry, I guess there's been some sort of a mistake," she said, beginning to turn away from the reservation desk.

"The mistake was mine," a deep voice said. "I made the reservation in my name," Jeff explained as he came up behind the hostess. Coming around the desk, he greeted Mikki with a warm smile. "I'm sorry, I should have told you that I put it in my name. Force of habit." Plucking a menu from the desk, his smile widened as he looked at her. "You came. I had my doubts."

"So did I," Mikki admitted in an unguarded moment.

He liked her honesty, he thought. Among other qualities. "Well, you're here now and you won't be sorry. I had to do a little bit of juggling," he told her, leading the way to a centrally located table, "but we have the best table in the restaurant."

"We?" Mikki asked. Her stomach tightened. On the way over, she'd almost talked herself into believing that he just wanted to have her here for dinner, but he'd be busy elsewhere.

"Yes, I'm eating with you," he explained. Then, rethinking the situation, he said, "Unless you'd rather I didn't."

She couldn't very well tell the man that she preferred eating alone, not without insulting him. Besides, this was his restaurant.

But she made one last attempt at a reprieve. "I thought you were very busy here."

"Happily, I am," he confirmed. "But I always felt that there was no lonelier feeling than eating alone in a room full of couples and families. Even the best food has a way of sticking to the roof of your mouth in that sort of situation. After what you did for my mother, the way you put her at ease and took care of her, not to mention saving her life, I wanted you to have the very best experience possible here." He held out her chair for her.

"And that's dining with you?" Mikki asked. Despite the mounting butterflies in her stomach, amusement curved the corners of her mouth as she asked the question.

Jeff took his seat opposite her. "Now that I play that back in my head, that does sound as if I'm rather full of myself, doesn't it?" he admitted with a self-deprecating laugh.

Mikki laughed softly, doing her best to relax. "No, that sounds rather thoughtful of you, really."

Opening the dark green menu, she took a moment to look over each of the four oversize pages with their long lists of appetizers and main courses. There were two more pages after that, one with a full spectrum of beverages and one offering an array of sinfully rich desserts.

There was just too much to choose from. It would be tomorrow before she could make up her mind. So, closing the menu, Mikki decided to leave the choice up to Jeff instead.

"So what's good here?" she finally asked, setting the menu on the table beside her.

He knew every item listed, was responsible for having created most of them. And while she had been studying the menu, he'd been covertly studying her. The subtle overhead lighting all but made love to her, highlighting her high cheekbones and smooth skin like a smitten teenager. Making her so beautiful, it almost hurt to look at her.

When she asked her question, the first response that occurred to him was one that he wasn't at liberty to voice.

You.

Instead, he gave her a choice between three main courses, all of which he could personally vouch for. Lobster bisque, veal scaloppini and, just for simplicity's sake, prime rib.

Rather than the lobster, she surprised him by going with something he'd always considered to be simple, but elegant.

"I'll have the prime rib—the small portion," Mikki added, since the meal came in three sizes.

"Wouldn't you rather order something a little more exotic?" he asked, thinking that perhaps she was being conservative in her choice on his account, because she didn't want it to seem as if she was taking advantage of his generosity.

"Actually, I'm a meat-and-potatoes kind of woman," she explained. "My mother always tended to order things like escargots, and anything that's better said in French, but I never developed a taste for any of that."

Mikki didn't add that she'd always thought her mother was being pretentious, because she never finished eating any of the complicated-sounding things that she ordered. "Most of the time," she said, "between studying in medical school and then working double and triple shifts interning at the hospital, I ate on the run, anyway. Once I was finally able to slow down a little bit, my tastes were already set in stone."

Jeff smiled at her, enjoying the fact that she had shared something personal with him, even if it just pertained to her acquired food preferences.

The server approached discreetly and took their order. Jeff waited until the woman withdrew before he said to Mikki, "Maybe I can talk you into having something a little more unique next time."

"Next time?" she repeated uncertainly. "You want to take me out to dinner again?"

She sounded somewhat uneasy. He wondered if it was his imagination, or if she felt that he was coming on too strong.

Leaning forward just a little, he said, "Doc, I have no doubts that if you hadn't treated my mother the way you did, with understanding and kindness, not to mention kid gloves, she never would have agreed to the operation. And if she hadn't, I'm pretty certain that instead of sitting across from a beautiful, highly skilled physician, at this moment I'd be seeing to my mother's funeral arrangements.

"What I am saying to you in a lot of words and none too clearly is that there is a table reserved for you at Dinner for Two for the rest of your life."

"I think you're getting a little carried away here," Mikki said with a self-conscious laugh.

He surprised her by saying, "Maybe." And then he added, "But it feels good to do this, so humor me. My mother, who my brother, my sister and I all love to death, is, quite notoriously, a handful. She is stubborn as the day is long and I can honestly say that I have never seen her managed so well and so effortlessly before."

Their food arrived far more quickly than she thought possible, and Mikki refrained from making a comment on his observation as she waited while the server placed their orders before them and then withdrew.

"This looks lovely," Mikki observed. Everything on both plates had been artistically arranged to please the eye as well as the palate.

"Half of every dining experience relies on visual appeal," he explained.

"And the other half is taste?" She'd expected him to say that it was *all* about taste and was surprised that he hadn't.

"Definitely," Jeff agreed with a grin. "The food can be made to look as pretty as humanly possible, but if it doesn't deliver in taste, the customers are not going to be coming back."

Listening to him, she took her first bite of the prime rib and immediately felt as if she had slipped into heaven.

Raising her eyes to his, she couldn't help commenting, "The customers are definitely coming back."

She meant it in general, but he took her remark to be specific and smiled at her. "I'm very glad to hear that."

Needing to do something about subduing the growing flutter in her stomach, Mikki went back to their previous topic of discussion. "I think your mother knew that something was wrong and she just needed someone to make her admit that, as well as make her feel that she could be helped."

"Well, all that is to your credit, because before you conducted your examination and talked with her, I had talked myself blue in the face trying to convince her to see a doctor. *Any* doctor," he confessed. "But time and again, she summarily refused. Because, as I mentioned to you in your office, my father was misdiagnosed, and when his condition did come to light, it was too late to treat him."

But Mikki had a different take on the situation. "Your mother wasn't resisting seeing a doctor because of what happened to your father. It was because, like so many patients suddenly faced with their own mortality, your mother was afraid."

"If she was afraid, wouldn't that make her *want* to get checked out quickly so whatever was wrong could be treated and taken care of?" he asked.

"You know how when a child closes their eyes, they think the world disappears because they can't see it? Well, it's kind of like that. If a person doesn't have that test and doesn't hear the doctor tell them that they have a specific disease or need to have something treated, then they don't have to deal with having to face the possible consequences.

"As long as what your mother was experiencing wasn't being given a specific name, she could go on pretending it didn't exist. That all that pain she kept having was due to gas, or indigestion, or just her imagination. Once a condition is given a name, it becomes real. And it becomes scarier."

Mikki looked down at her plate and suddenly realized that she had talked while eating the prime rib and baked potato she'd ordered. Her plate was absolutely clean.

"I'm sorry," she apologized. "I just talked shop all the way through dinner."

He found her delightful. "First off, don't be sorry. I was the one who asked you questions, and I did find your explanation to be enlightening. And second, you didn't talk all the way through dinner. There's still a lot more dinner left to go," he promised.

"More?" Mikki repeated, her eyes widening as she looked at the man sitting across from her. "But I'm stuffed."

"Ah, but there's always room for dessert," he told her, laughing. "And," he qualified, "you certainly don't have to eat it right away. We can linger for the rest of the evening if you'd like," he assured her. And then, leaning in, he lowered his voice and said with a straight face, "I know the man who owns this place. We don't have to eat and run."

Sitting back again, Jeff asked her, "Would you care for some wine? Or a cordial? Or perhaps something light and fruity to drink?"

"Coffee," she told him automatically. It was an easy choice.

"Coffee?" he repeated uncertainly. At this hour, most people preferred to have a drink rather than something that would keep them awake.

Mikki nodded. "I need to keep my head clear," she explained, "just in case I get a call from the hospital."

"Are you expecting a call from the hospital?" he questioned, beginning to realize the full extent of the life she led. What she told him next confirmed it.

"I'm *always* expecting a call from the hospital," Mikki said. "Almost all doctors do—unless they happen to specialize in dermatology," she added with a touch of humor. "Dermatologists are the ones who get to keep regular hours."

"But I take it that you don't?" Jeff asked. From where he was sitting, it seemed to be a rhetorical question.

She didn't want him thinking she was trying to look like some sort of a martyr. "For the most part, I do. But there have been cases..." she allowed. "Like when a patient's ulcer decided to perforate just before midnight on Christmas Eve."

"Christmas Eve?" he repeated. "That had to be hard on you."

She didn't want him thinking that she had told him the story so he could feel sorry for her. It was just to illustrate how unpredictable her vocation was.

"Not really," she told him, backtracking. "I had no plans."

"Then you don't celebrate Christmas," Jeff guessed.

"No, I do. Usually with my best friend and her family," she qualified. "But for the most part, I usually sub for the doctors who want to be home with their families on Christmas."

"No family, then?" he asked, finding himself wanting to know things about this beautiful woman with the very sad eyes.

"I have a family—" Stopping abruptly, she looked up at him. "How did we get started talking about this?"

"One word led to another," he told her innocently. For now, not wanting to spook her, he backed off. "I guess I've got the kind of face that most people like to talk to."

That might very well be true, except that she didn't usually like to talk, Mikki thought. At least not about herself.

Still, she had to admit, she was enjoying herself.

Chapter Eleven

"Do you actually expect me to eat that?"

Mikki looked at the large slice of tiramisu cake on the plate in front of her. The meal she'd just consumed had been more than filling, and she doubted there was even a tiny bit of space left in her stomach.

"It's huge," she protested, adding, "If I eat it, I'll explode."

"It's not as big as you think," Jeff assured her, "and I can personally vouch for the fact that it really does melt in your mouth. But all I'm asking is that you try a single forkful to see if you like it. If you do, you can take the rest of it home with you. That's why God created doggie bags," he added with a grin.

She looked at the dessert, a light, fluffy serving of mousse and whipped cream trapped between several paper-thin layers of confection—and she had to admit that it did look absolutely delicious.

"I guess I can manage to fit in one small bite," Mikki speculated.

He held the dessert fork out to her.

After a moment, she took it.

"But if I explode all over you," she warned, "you can't blame me."

"I never blame a patron," Jeff told her solemnly. "It's bad for business and word like that gets around very quickly."

Mikki had never been the type to overindulge—and that included overeating—not even as a child. So despite the cake's very tempting appearance, she was ready for this to be a less than pleasant experience.

Bracing herself, she slid the side of her fork into the cake before her. Then gingerly bringing the fork to her lips, she opened her mouth and then closed it again around the sliver she'd separated from the rest of her dessert.

Mikki was prepared to become almost nauseated because she felt she was literally stuffing herself.

However, she discovered that Jeff was right. The sample was so light and airy, it was as if she'd closed her mouth over a thought, an impression, an illusion of cake, but not anything that was real and certainly not substantial.

She looked up to find Jeff watching her. He seemed like a kid at Christmas, waiting to find out if Santa was real, the way he believed, or not real, the way everyone else maintained.

She found the expression on his face touching almost against her will.

"Well?" he asked when Mikki said nothing.

A sigh of pleasure escaped her lips. "You're right.

This is fantastic. But I'm still taking it home with me—if your offer still stands."

"Absolutely," he told her enthusiastically.

"Because I just can't do it justice here." She felt obligated to explain. "I *am* very full. More than full, actually."

"I understand perfectly." Turning, he signaled the young woman who had served them their dinner. She was at their table almost instantly. "Rachel, please box this up for Dr. McKenna—and put an extra piece in the box, please."

"Yes, sir," the young woman said, all but snapped to attention.

The man was going over and above the call, Mikki couldn't help thinking. "Are you sure I can't pay for any of this?" Mikki asked him. She'd glimpsed the prices on the menu when she'd perused it earlier, and they were far from inexpensive.

"I thought I made it clear that your money's not good here. And that you're welcome here anytime."

Was he issuing her a standing invitation? "I don't get a chance to get out much," she began, about to demur his offer.

But Jeff deftly headed her off at the pass.

"All the more reason to come here and eat. I know you eat," he stressed with a smile. "Like a bird, but you eat. And based on my own experience, I can testify that getting out once in a while is good for the soul—not to mention that it allows you to recharge your batteries."

"Well, my batteries—and my soul—are sufficiently recharged, so I'd better get going and free this table up for one of your other patrons. Your *paying* patrons," she stressed. Turning, she looked past the reservation desk.

There were an awful lot of people there, all waiting for tables. "I can see a line forming."

Jeff laughed, rising to his feet. "They're not all waiting for *our* table. However, I'm happy to say that business is very good."

"Well, it should be," she answered, surprising him. "The food certainly is."

He executed a little bow. "Thank you."

Mikki returned the courtesy by inclining her head in a gesture of thanks. "And thank you for dinner."

"Anytime," he said, then repeated, "*Any*time." Picking up the boxed dessert, he told her, "I'll walk you out."

She wanted to tell him that he didn't have to do that, that she knew he had to be very busy. But for some reason, maybe because she *had* had a good time, the words didn't come out.

Instead, she decided to let Jeff walk her to the entrance of the restaurant—or the exit, depending on her viewpoint. Besides, this whole dinner had been a one-time thing, and as such, she'd decided to simply enjoy it for what it was and leave it at that.

Her life was a whirlwind of patients and the hospital, not to mention her volunteer work at the free clinic. She was always giving a hundred and ten percent of herself. Just this once, she decided to have a little me time, and as such, she intended to savor it—especially since it was almost over.

But like Cinderella holding her lone glass slipper after the ball ended, she had her souvenir of a surprisingly happy evening—she had her cake.

"Where's your car?" Jeff asked as they reached the double doors.

"Outside," she answered.

He laughed. "Considering the alternative, my insurance agent will be very happy to hear that. *Where* outside?"

She thought for a moment. She'd been in a hurry to park and have Nikki go on her way, she hadn't really paid that much attention to the exact spot. "Um, I'm not sure," she admitted.

"Well, then let's go look for it," Jeff offered, opening the double door and holding it for her.

She didn't feel right about this.

"I've monopolized you long enough," Mikki protested. "I can't take you away from your work any longer."

"Doc, it's dark out," he pointed out as they stepped outside. "I know this is Bedford and it's usually incredibly safe, but there's always that one in a million chance that someone might want to take advantage of a beautiful woman under the cover of night. Humor me and let me walk you to your car."

A rush of warmth came over her, and it had nothing to do with the fact that it was an early spring evening. She did her best to block it out.

"I know you don't do this for all your patrons," she insisted.

"No, you're right," he agreed. "But, like the name of my restaurant implies, most of my patrons come here to dine in pairs. And, in addition, none of my patrons saved my mother's life."

Mikki felt herself weakening despite her attempts to remain strong. "You make it very hard to argue with you," she told him.

Jeff's eyes appeared darker in this light, and they

seemed to almost sparkle as he smiled at her. "Good. Now, what color is your car?" he asked, looking around.

"It's a light blue Corolla. It's a two-door," she added.

"Right, I remember now. Two doors," he repeated. "That's why we took my car when we drove my mother to the hospital."

The parking lot was filled to capacity, and it took several minutes before they were able to locate her car. Ironically, Jeff was the one to spot it first.

"Is it that one?" he asked, pointing at a nearby vehicle.

She felt like an idiot for not having seen it first—and for forgetting where she had parked in the first place.

"Yes, that's it," Mikki told him. "Okay," she declared, taking the boxed tiramisu from his hands. Her fingers accidentally brushed against his, and something seemed to momentarily stir within her. "I can take it from here. Thank you again," she said, all but tossing the words over her shoulder as she hurried away.

She moved fast, he thought, wondering if it was because she was afraid that he would try to kiss her. He had to admit that it was a tempting thought, but one he would have never acted on unless she gave him some sort of indication that she wanted him to.

He stood there, watching her go, then waited until she got into the car. Not because he thought anything might happen to her. No, he watched just because he found the view to be extremely appealing from where he was standing.

Maybe what he was feeling *was* motivated by gratitude. At this point he really couldn't honestly say. But he did know that there was something about this graceful, beautiful woman with the appealing mouth that moved him and made him smile—from the inside out.

He stayed where he was until he saw her open her car door and get in. After Mikki pulled out of the lot, he finally turned around and went back inside. And that, Jeff mused, was the closest he'd come to a date in two years. Maybe he needed to begin delegating more so he could do this again—and this time bring his date home. After all, he'd been gone the whole day when his mother had had her surgery earlier this week and the world hadn't come to an end—and neither had his restaurant.

Pausing to take his wallet out of his back pocket, he fished through it. Nestled between the various business cards, he found what he was looking for—the card he'd picked up when he'd initially brought his mother to the doctor's office.

The woman's name was written in bold script. *Michelle McKenna, MD.*

The corners of his mouth curved as he stood looking down at the card.

Maybe.

Well, she'd survived, Mikki thought. She had gone to Jeff's restaurant, had dinner with the man and, if pressed, she was even willing to say that it had been a rather pleasant experience.

However, it had been a onetime experience and there was no reason to dwell on it, no reason to start daydreaming and fashioning castles in the sky, she silently insisted.

Most of all, she wasn't her mother, Mikki reminded herself. Her mother, who turned every minor encounter with a man into the greatest get-together since Scarlett and Rhett first met in *Gone With the Wind*.

Or maybe, she reevaluated, for her mother, every encounter she had actually *was* that sort of a get-together, because everyone knew how that particular love story ended. The same way all her mother's so-called love stories did: in total disaster.

"Your problem, Mother," Mikki said aloud to the thought of the woman who was undoubtedly letting her hair down at some party or other at this very moment, looking for her next ex-husband-to-be, "is that you never quit while you were ahead. Never called it a night, picked up your chips and went home. You weren't happy until you were on some man's arm—and eventually you weren't happy there, either," she murmured, parking her car in her driveway.

"My way is better. Lonelier, maybe," Mikki allowed. "But better."

Besides, she thought, letting herself into her house, her mother's liaisons never lasted and Veronica wound up alone anyway. Her own way was better. No false hopes, no brutal letdowns.

No one at all.

She had just enough time to kick off her shoes before her phone rang. Mikki approached the landline warily, like a lion tamer checking out his lion's mood before proceeding into the arena.

The caller ID told her that it was Nikki calling, undoubtedly to find out how everything had gone. Picking up the receiver, Mikki flopped down on the sofa, the way she had as a teenager.

"How did you know I just got in?" she asked without bothering to utter any cursory greeting first.

She heard her friend laugh. "Because I'm psychic, because you and I are spiritually connected—and because I've been calling every ten minutes and this is the first time that you've picked up," Nikki told her. "So, how was it?"

Pretty good, really. *Really* good. Out loud she answered guardedly, "It was okay."

"Just okay?"

Mikki heard the disappointment in her friend's voice. For some reason, seeing her go out with someone seemed to mean a lot to Nikki. And because it obviously did, she stopped behaving as if having dinner with Jeff Sabatino was no different than a quick, detached visit to the local hardware store.

"Maybe better than okay," Mikki allowed quietly after a beat.

But that wasn't enough for Nikki. "How much better?"

Mikki sighed. She might as well find out exactly what she was up against. "Just what are you trying to get me to say, Dr. Sommers?"

"I just want you to tell me the truth, Mikki," her friend answered. "That's all. Just the truth."

"All right," Mikki said. "The truth is that the dinner was fantastic, the restaurant was fabulous. And Jeff was very attentive. We talked all through the meal without realizing that time was just melting away and I want you to be the first to know that I'm having his baby."

"You're what?" Nikki cried, momentarily taken aback. And then she obviously realized that the other woman was putting her on. "Oh, right. Very funny, Mikki." She sighed, disappointed. "So I take it that you *didn't* have a good time."

Well, there was no point in lying. Their friendship was based on the truth and mutual respect.

"No, actually, if you must know, I did. Jeff was…" Mikki hunted for the right word, but in a moment of self-preservation, she finally decided to settle on, "Nice."

"Nice?" Nikki echoed incredulously. "Bacon and eggs are nice. Was that man just plain old bacon and eggs, Mikki, or was he more like caviar?"

"Neither," Mikki answered, then because Nikki was her best friend and had always been there for her through some very rough times with her mother, she found herself sighing before reluctantly admitting, "He was prime rib."

Nikki knew how her friend felt about prime rib. It constituted her very favorite meal in the whole world. A feeling of triumph flooded through her. Her mother had come through. "Even better," she declared, pleased.

"Can we drop this, please?" Mikki requested, uncomfortable with the way the conversation was going. "I have surgery first thing tomorrow morning and I'd like to get some sleep so I'm not bleary-eyed when I'm cutting into Mr. Miller."

"You're doing it again," Nikki told her. "You're coming up with excuses so you don't have to take a long, hard look at your feelings."

"My feelings are tired now, which means I might wind up saying things I shouldn't," Mikki warned her.

"Okay, I'll let you go for now. But we'll talk again later," Nikki told her.

Mikki groaned before hanging up. Loudly.

Chapter Twelve

The operation went without a hitch, despite the fact that her patient was nearly a hundred pounds over-weight and that made removing his gallstones particularly challenging.

For the most part, Mikki preferred the surgical procedures that she undertook to be straightforward. She ordinarily liked her challenges to come in the form of difficult crossword puzzles.

However, she was grateful for anything that kept her mind occupied and off other things. Specifically off a strikingly handsome restaurateur.

The moment her gallstone patient was wheeled off to the recovery room, Mikki hurried to the locker room so she could change out of her scrubs.

Because of the patient's extra weight, the surgery had run long. What that meant was that she had exactly fifteen minutes to change and get over to her office before her office hours started.

She made it with approximately a minute and a half to spare. "Wow, just in time," Molly said, only moderately startled by Mikki's appearance. "So, how did Mr. Miller's operation go?"

Taking off her jacket, Mikki put on her lab coat. "It ran long, but I'm happy to report that both patient and doctor survived the ordeal," she answered.

"Well, I'm glad that *you* survived, because you've got a waiting room full of patients," Virginia told her, coming out of the third exam room. "By the way," she asked, dropping her voice, "how did dinner go last night?"

Mikki didn't bother asking her head nurse how she knew about the dinner. Somehow, Virginia always managed to ferret things out long before they ever became public knowledge.

Instead, Mikki merely answered, "Appetizing."

Virginia grinned wickedly. "Are you talking about the meal or the man?"

Mikki decided that it was best not to answer that question, or even acknowledge it. She focused on her patients.

"Who's first?" she asked her receptionist.

"That would be Mrs. Watters," Angela answered. "She's in exam room one."

"Got it," Mikki said, picking up the top file. And she was off.

The pace from that moment on was nonstop without a letup, partially because there had been two unscheduled patients wedged in, in addition to all the other patients already in her waiting room. Each of the two had called the office, pleading to be fit in. However, her day was jam-packed, predominantly because Mikki never moved on to the next patient until the one she was with was completely satisfied that all of his or her questions had been answered. Anything less was unthinkable to Mikki.

She didn't stop going until well after three o'clock, at which point she ate half a salad before resuming her examinations again.

By six thirty that evening, Mikki felt drained, but at least all of her patients had been seen to. Her *office* patients.

She breathed a sigh of relief. The finish line was in sight.

All that was left to do was to check in on her patient from that morning's surgery. If he was doing well, she'd be free to go home. No one had called from the hospital to inform her that there was any sort of a problem with Mr. Miller, but while hopeful, Mikki never took anything for granted.

"How do you do it?" Molly marveled just as she was about to leave the office herself.

"It's the glamour," Mikki deadpanned. "It keeps me going."

And then, telling her staff "Good night," she hurried off to see her last patient of the day. Mr. Miller, the nurse on duty on his floor told her, was doing very well. Quickly reviewing the man's chart to verify the verbal report, Mikki went into her patient's room and found him sleeping comfortably.

Satisfied, Mikki finally called it a day.

By the time she arrived home, parked her car and

got out, she felt so exhausted she could barely put one foot in front of the other.

Closing the door behind her, she was halfway to her kitchen when she remembered that she had never gotten around to going to the supermarket that week. The only thing in her refrigerator besides a third of a loaf of bread and a bottle of rosé, thanks to her mother's visit a couple of months ago, was a small basket of strawberries. The basket was half-full. Unfortunately for her, the strawberries had turned and were well on their way to becoming inedible.

Mikki tried to be philosophical about it. "I need to lose a few pounds, anyway," she murmured.

Besides, she needed sleep more than she needed food. She had just crossed the living room and was on her way to the stairs and her bedroom upstairs when her cell phone rang.

Muttering a fragment of a prayer, she sincerely hoped it wasn't her mother or someone calling because they had what they felt constituted an emergency. Hungry and tired, she was definitely not at her diplomatic peak right now.

She didn't recognize the number on her phone, and the only clue she had were the words *out of area* over the phone number.

Taking a chance, she picked up the receiver anyway. "This is Dr. McKenna."

"Did I get you at a bad time?"

The voice was deep, rich and she thought she knew who it belonged to, but just in case, she said, "I'm sorry, who's this?"

"Oh, I thought my name showed up on your screen. Sorry. This is Jeff Sabatino."

"Is something wrong with your mother?" she asked, immediately concerned. She struggled not to allow her heart to leap around wildly the way it had begun to do and forced her mind to focus on the practical reason for his call.

She had discharged Sophia from the hospital two days ago. It would have been sooner, but she had kept his mother in an extra day because of her age. She wanted to make sure the woman had fully recovered enough to go home safely.

Ideally, Sophia wasn't due for a recheck for another week, but Mikki knew that things didn't always go according to plan. Mentally, she crossed her fingers as she waited for Jeff's answer.

"No, nothing like that," Jeff quickly assured her. "Mom's staying at my sister Tina's house for a couple of weeks until she gets her strength back, but she's doing fine thanks to you. I'm calling because I was just wondering if perhaps you'd like to stop by the restaurant on Saturday for another meal, since apparently there were no ill effects from the last one."

"Saturday?" Mikki repeated to make sure she'd heard him correctly. When he didn't contradict her, she said, "I'm sorry. I'd love to, but I can't. Saturday's my day at the free clinic."

"The free clinic. You volunteer there?" Jeff asked. She hadn't mentioned that before, but it didn't surprise him. The more he knew about her, the more selfless this woman seemed.

"It's something I got into when I was in medical school," Mikki explained. "And I guess that I just never stopped going—except that now I'm a licensed doctor instead of just a medical student and they let me do doctor stuff," she added wryly. She heard him chuckle softly. The sound pleased her—more than it should have. Red flags went up. She needed to be wary, she told herself. "I'm sorry. Maybe some other time."

And then, unable to stop herself, Mikki yawned. Audibly. Embarrassed, she quickly told him, "Oh, Lord, I'm sorry. I didn't mean to yawn. That wasn't because of you. It's just that it's been a very, very long day.," she assured him.

"Well, then I won't keep you," Jeff told her. "I just wanted you to know that I was serious about that open invitation."

"I appreciate it," she told him. Then, because she didn't want Jeff to think that she was just trying to get rid of him, she said, "I don't know if I told you yesterday evening, but I think that you have a very nice restaurant."

"Thanks." And then he asked, "Can I quote you on that?"

He'd caught her off guard again. Was the man talking about getting her to give him an endorsement for his establishment? "Excuse me?"

He heard the nervous uncertainty in her voice. "I'm just kidding, Doc. Go to bed," he told her. And then he added, "Good night, Doc," just before he terminated the call.

She was a grown woman with medical degrees in several fields. There was no reason for her to feel this odd, giddy, fluttery feeling just because she'd gotten an unexpected call from a man she barely knew.

A nice man, she qualified, but still one she barely knew.

She went up the stairs smiling.

* * *

Over the course of the next week, Mikki found herself thinking about Jeff's call a number of times. More than once she caught herself wishing that her Saturdays weren't spoken for.

But they were, and she knew what she did was vital. She was performing a much-needed service because for some of the people she saw at the clinic, she was their only contact with the medical world.

As luck would have it, this particular Saturday the clinic was severely understaffed. Except for one retired nurse, Frieda Halpert, Mikki was the only medical person on duty at the clinic. The other doctor and the two other nurses who were usually there had called at the last minute to say they wouldn't be in. All of them had family matters to deal with. When it rained, it poured, Mikki couldn't help thinking.

As usual, the waiting room was filled to capacity when she walked in that Saturday morning. Appointments weren't necessary at the clinic. The usual procedure was that people came in when they needed to.

Mikki felt like the last woman standing two minutes after she'd walked in. Rolling up her sleeves, she declared, "Let's get started," to Frieda and she dived in.

Two hours into her day, she felt as if she had barely made a dent. For every patient she saw, it seemed like two more came in.

At this rate, she would be here into the wee hours of the night. And the noise from the waiting room, despite Frieda's efforts, just kept getting louder. One of the children had been crying nonstop for what seemed like an hour, growing progressively louder.

And then, abruptly, the noise stopped.

Completely.

Finished with the patient she'd just examined, Mikki looked quizzically at the veteran nurse. "Did they all leave?" she asked.

"We wouldn't be that lucky." Holding up her finger, Frieda went out into the waiting room to check. When she returned, there was a bemused expression on her well-lined face.

"No, nobody left," Frieda reported. "They're just being fed."

"Excuse me?"

Frieda jerked a thumb toward the front of the clinic. "There's a guy out in the waiting area and he's handing out a boatload of food."

"We're done here, Mr. Willis," Mikki told the older man whose bandage she had just changed. "That gives you any trouble—" she indicated his arm "—I'll see you here next week. Come in sooner if you need to."

"You gonna be here all week?" the older man asked.

"No, I'll be here on Saturday," she told him. "Same as always."

He nodded his shaky gray head. "Then I'll come back Saturday."

She accepted the compliment. "I'll see you then." And then, unable to hold back any longer, she hurried out to the waiting room to find out just what was going on.

When she walked out into the waiting area to look around, Mikki was convinced that her imagination had just run away with her. There was no other explanation for why Jeff was there, handing out a ton of boxed lunches he had apparently brought in using a large dolly.

"Jeff?" she asked uncertainly, coming closer.

He turned his head in her direction and flashed that unmistakable sexy grin at her. No doubt about it, the man was too good-looking for her own good. "Hi."

"What are you doing here?" she asked. Realizing that her question sounded almost hostile, she did her best to amend her tone. "I mean, not that it's not nice to see you, but—what are you doing here?" she asked again, totally confused.

A pint-size girl with curly blond hair ran up to Mikki and tugged on her lab coat to get her attention. When Mikki looked down at the girl—whom she recognized, because her mother had brought her in several times—Eva unabashedly asked, "Is he your boyfriend, Dr. Mikki?"

Blindsided, Mikki practically stuttered as she answered, "No, he's, um—"

"I'm a friend of the doc's," Jeff said, coming to her rescue. "She made my mother well a couple of weeks ago," he told the little girl. "The doc works so hard she keeps forgetting to eat, so I thought I'd bring her some food."

"But why did you bring so much food?" Eva asked, fisting her small hands on her waist as she surveyed the many boxes. "She can't eat all that."

"No, she can't," he agreed. "But she doesn't like to eat alone and she knew there'd be a lot of people in her waiting room, so she asked me to bring enough food for everyone."

"Oh." Eva thought the answer over and her face lit up. "That's good. Can my mom eat some?"

"Everyone can have some," Jeff replied. "That's why I brought so much. Would you like to help me hand the boxes out?"

The little girl bobbed her head up and down, her curls bouncing every which way. "Sure. I like helping. Don't I, Mama?" She looked toward her mother for backup.

A worn woman, looking far more tired than her years warranted, nodded and smiled at her daughter. "Yes, you do."

Mikki looked on in amazement, wondering what had possessed Jeff Sabatino to do this.

But very quickly, she stopped looking for a reason and was just happy that he had thought to do something so magnanimous.

Leaving the waiting room, Mikki got back to work.

Mikki expected Jeff to leave after he had distributed the last of the food and everyone had eaten. Instead, he came into the inner office and surprised her by asking, "Mind if I hang around until you close up tonight?"

Although she had to admit that she liked having him there, Mikki didn't want him feeling obligated to stay.

"It might be a while," she warned.

He shrugged. "That's okay. I left the restaurant in my assistant's hands and my mother is with my sister, so basically I'm free," he told her. "So, is it okay with you?"

"It's fine with me," she answered, wishing that she could think of something witty to say. But she came up empty.

Getting back to work, she wasn't able to quell the flutter in her stomach, so she decided just to ignore it, focusing on the patients waiting for her attention.

It felt like forever, but eventually, the last of the patients left the clinic and Frieda quickly closed the doors.

"Well, I've got a cat and a husband to get home to and make dinner for," she announced in her typical no-nononsense voice. "Nice of you to come by and feed the masses," she told Jeff, nodding as she picked up her things and made her way to the back door.

Then, passing Mikki, she said to the doctor in a low voice, "You want my opinion, he's a keeper."

"He's not mine to keep," Mikki quickly protested.

"Uh-huh," Frieda replied, sounding completely unconvinced.

Turning at the door, she glanced over her shoulder at the man who had come in and disrupted everything at the clinic, but in a very good way. "Hope to see you again, Mr. Sabatino."

"Jeff," he corrected her.

Frieda's uneven smile widened with approval. "Jeff," she repeated. "A keeper," she told Mikki again just before she let herself out.

Chapter Thirteen

"Looks like you have a fan," Mikki told him once they were alone. She saw Jeff raise an eyebrow as he looked at her. Afraid that he might have misunderstood her meaning, she quickly explained, "I was talking about Frieda."

"I see. But not you."

His expression was unreadable. Had she insulted him, or hurt his feelings? She didn't want to do that, but she didn't want to say too much, either. While she was attracted to him, she didn't want to encourage him, because that way lay trouble. She'd learned that by watching her mother.

"I like your food," she told Jeff. "And I admire your generous spirit."

He nodded, accepting her rather vague compliments. He didn't want her to feel as if he was crowding her. "I've been told worse things," he allowed.

"I'm just trying to figure out why you would come here and bring all this food with you."

"Well, it's simple," he told her. He watched as she began closing everything down. "I came here because you were here. I brought the food because you seemed to enjoy it the other evening."

"You brought way too much food," she told him and he knew it.

"Actually," Jeff corrected, "it turned out that I brought just enough. You had an awful lot of patients here, not to mention that most of them didn't come here alone."

"So you *did* plan on feeding all these people?" she questioned incredulously. Who *did* that kind of thing?

Jeff explained his reasoning. "I knew you wouldn't eat unless they had something to eat, too. Luckily, I'm in a position where bringing extra food with me is not a problem."

Mikki looked at this surprising philanthropist, still not a hundred percent clear about what had gone through his head—or how he would even think to do something like this.

"I don't understand. How would you even know—"

"My dad died when I was very young. I was raised by a single mom who sometimes had to work two jobs to make ends meet and feed all of us. And, as a kid, I wasn't a stranger to free clinics." He glanced around at the area that had been teeming with people just a short while ago. "Let's just say that this is payback—on a small scale."

She had just assumed that he had come from a comfortable background. To find out differently surprised her. "I didn't know."

He laughed. There was no reason why she would. "I don't have it printed on the back of the menus, but it's not a secret, either," he told her. "So," Jeff said, changing the subject. "Does this mean you're done for the day?"

"It's after eight o'clock. The clinic is officially closed," she told him. She began to turn off the overhead lights as she slowly made her way to the back.

"Considering it's strictly on a volunteer basis, you certainly put in long hours here," Jeff commented.

He was telling her that he thought she was being overworked. Right now, considering the way she felt, she couldn't really argue with him. But she felt she needed to tell him that it wasn't always this hectic here.

"There's normally another doctor here, too. We take shifts. I open the place and he closes up."

He nodded, taking it in. He'd been here for half the day and the only medical personnel he'd seen were Mikki and the dour-faced nurse. "And where is he?"

"He had a family emergency—same as the two other nurses who are usually here," she added.

He nodded. "I see. So in other words, it was all on your shoulders."

Mikki raised her chin somewhat defensively. "I managed."

"Yes, you certainly did," Jeff agreed. The last thing he wanted to do was offend her or get in some sort of an argument over the nature of her rather zealous work ethic. "Could I interest you in going back to the restaurant for a drink, or some dessert?" he asked her. He really wanted to spend some time with this compelling woman in a somewhat less harried setting.

She considered his offer. "Either one sounds good."

Jeff grinned. "Either one it is."

But just as she was about to turn off the last two lights in the clinic, there was a loud pounding on the front door. Surprised, Mikki immediately turned toward the front of the clinic.

But Jeff was apparently leerier than she was. He quickly moved in front of her, blocking her access to the door.

"Don't open that," he warned her. "Your hours are posted outside. Everyone knows that the clinic is closed now, and this isn't the greatest neighborhood," he pointed out.

Whoever it was pounded on the door again. "That sounds like someone who needs help," Mikki argued.

"If they need help, there's a hospital a few blocks away," he reminded her.

The pounding started again, even more urgent sounding than the last two times. Moving him out of the way, Mikki undid all three locks and opened the door just enough to be able to look out. There was a distraught woman on the other side, holding a whimpering little boy of no more than five in her arms.

The second the door was opened, the woman began talking. "Please, my son, I think he broke his arm. He needs help." The woman looked at Jeff, directing her words to him. "You're the doctor, right?" she asked breathlessly.

"No, she's the doctor," he said, indicating Mikki. "Here, let me help you," he offered, taking the bruised little boy from the woman.

At this point, the child, clearly frightened, began to cry and moan as he shrank away from Jeff.

"Bring him in the back," Mikki instructed him. She paused only long enough to lock the door again. "The first room," she called out to Jeff. "Put him on the exam table."

"I wanna go home," the boy cried.

Mikki was quick to follow in Jeff's wake. The boy's mother was one step behind.

"You will, sweetie," Mikki told him. "I just want to take a look at that arm."

Obviously anticipating more pain, the boy was wiggling as he sat on the exam table. It made things difficult and each time the boy moved, he whimpered and cried.

"Jeff, could you help him stay still?" Mikki requested. "Jeff's going to play statue with you," she told the little boy. "Both of you are going to stay as still as possible." She smiled encouragingly at him. "I bet you'll win, too."

"Mama?" the boy cried, looking toward his mother for help.

"Listen to the nice doctor, Henry," his mother told him, clearly on the verge of tears herself. Worry lines were permanently imprinted on her forehead.

"But she's gonna hurt me," Henry cried.

"Oh, you must be thinking of some other doctor, Henry," Jeff told the boy. "Dr. Mikki never hurts anyone." He winked at Henry. "*Especially* if you stay very, very still."

"Like a statue?" Henry asked, trying to look brave enough, though a few tears escaped and were sliding down his cheeks.

"Just like a statue," Jeff told him solemnly. He raised his eyes to Mikki's. "We're ready."

"All right, Henry," Mikki began in a calm, sooth-ing voice, "I'm going to have to examine your arm—"

Henry immediately froze up. "No!" he protested.

"Why don't we have Dr. Mikki examine my arm first?" Jeff suggested. "Then you can see that she's not going to hurt you."

The boy looked at him uncertainly, as if trying to decide whether or not to trust him. Finally, he sniffed, "Okay."

"I'm ready, Doc," Jeff told her, pretending to brace himself for the boy's benefit.

Mikki went through the motions, slowly feeling up and down Jeff's outstretched arm. Henry was watching her so intently, she could almost feel his eyes on her.

"No break here," Mikki concluded. She moved away from Jeff and turned toward the little boy. "All right, it's your turn, Henry."

Henry stayed exactly where he was. Instead, he looked at Jeff. "Did it hurt?"

Jeff shook his head. "Maybe a little, but not too much," he answered, knowing that if he said no, the lit-tle boy would immediately balk at the first sign of pain.

"Henry, the doctor has to look at your arm," his mother told him. The woman turned toward Mikki. "He was running and he fell right on it. When I touched it, he started screaming. He's so delicate," Henry's mother added. "He's always been that way."

The woman looked as if she was very close to burst-ing into tears.

"Looks like a big, strong boy to me," Jeff observed. Henry gave him a grateful, brave smile. "What do you think, Dr. Mikki?"

"I agree," Mikki answered, giving the boy an encouraging smile. "This'll be over with really quickly," she promised.

She watched the boy brace himself. Very gently, she passed her fingers along the upper portion of his arm—the part she knew hadn't been hurt.

Henry watched her with huge eyes. And then, startled, he stifled a yelp of pain as she worked her way down his forearm.

"It hurts, it hurts!" he yelled. He would have pulled back his arm if Jeff hadn't been holding it down, keeping the limb immobile.

"I know it does, sweetheart, but you're being really, really brave and we'll be finished soon." She looked at Jeff, silently asking for his help. "I'm going to have to take an X-ray."

"What's that?" Henry cried, looking really frightened.

"That's a picture of your bones," she explained soothingly. "You've had pictures taken, haven't you, Henry?"

"Sometimes," he answered warily, watching her every move again.

"Tell you what, pal," Jeff said. "How about I take you to where the doc has her X-ray machine and she'll take that picture of your arm in no time?"

Henry looked up at him, clearly wavering. "You'll be there, too?"

"Wouldn't miss it for the world," Jeff told the boy. "Ready?" he asked, coming over to stand next to the exam table.

Henry nodded. "Ready."

As gently as possible, Jeff picked the boy up and,

with Mikki leading the way, he brought the boy into the room where the X-rays were taken.

At the hospital, this was something that was done by the technicians. But Mikki had watched it being done often enough to feel confident that she could operate the X-ray machine herself.

With Jeff's help, she managed to take two views of the break in Henry's arm. Development of the films went quickly.

"That doesn't look like my arm," Henry protested when Mikki showed him the X-rays he'd asked to see.

"That's what it looks like under your skin. See this tiny line here?" she asked, pointing it out to the boy as if she was talking to a colleague.

Henry leaned forward, squinting hard as he looked at the X-ray. "Uh-huh."

"That's called a hairline fracture," she told him. "That's what you have."

A terrified expression came over his face. "Is my arm going to fall off?"

Mikki congratulated herself for not laughing. "No, honey, we're going to put a cast on it and it'll be good as new in a few weeks."

"In the meantime, you'll have this cool cast all your friends are going to want to sign," Jeff told him.

Henry twisted around on the exam table to look up at his new friend. "They can't write."

Undaunted, Jeff switched gears. "They'll draw pictures."

Henry nodded. "Okay." Reassured, he turned so that he was looking up at the doctor. "Do it."

"You've got a brave guy here, Mrs. Hendricks," Mikki said to the boy's mother.

The woman nodded, blinking back tears of relief. "I know."

Working methodically, Mikki prepared the plaster for the cast and applied it, layer by layer, onto the boy's arm. She made sure she used a material that dried very quickly.

"It's kinda heavy," Henry told her when she was finished, gingerly lifting his arm up.

"I know, but that's to make sure your bone grows together," Mikki told him.

Turning away, she opened up the bottom drawer in the cast room cabinet. After some rummaging, she found what she was looking for.

"Here, let's put this sling on. It'll help distribute the weight for you." She slipped the sling, which had little cartoon characters on it, onto his arm and then up, onto the back of his neck. "There you go. You're all set." Turning toward the boy's mother, she told her, "I'm going to need to see him in two weeks. Depending on how it goes, we can put a lighter cast on in its place at that time."

"More casts?" Henry groaned.

"But it'll be lighter," Mikki emphasized, smiling at him.

"And your friends can draw more pictures," Jeff told the boy.

Henry glanced down at his cast. "Yeah, they can, can't they?" That seemed to satisfy him.

Jeff helped the boy off the exam table. His mother turned toward Mikki.

"How much do I owe you?" Mrs. Hendricks asked. The lines on her face seemed to deepen as she fumbled inside her purse.

Mikki put her hand over the other woman's, stilling it. When the woman raised her eyes in question, Mikki told the boy's mother, "It's called a free clinic for a reason."

Mrs. Hendricks exhaled a huge breath. "I don't know how to thank you," she said, tears shining in her eyes. A couple slid down her cheeks.

"Just teach him to walk, not run, and we'll call it even," Mikki quipped.

"Don't worry," she said, putting her arm around her son's shoulders—she had to stoop a little to do it. "I'm not letting him out of my sight."

"He was just being a kid," Jeff said, coming to Henry's defense. "Weren't you, Henry? Kids break things, sometimes on their own bodies. It happens. But you're going to try to be more careful, aren't you?" he asked.

The boy bobbed his head up and down. "Uh-huh. For sure."

"Good enough for me," Jeff responded, ruffling the boy's hair. "Can I drop you two off at your home?" he offered, turning toward Mrs. Hendricks.

"No, that's all right, really. It's just a few blocks away from here," Mrs. Hendricks told him. "We can walk."

"Yes, but riding in a car is faster. Besides, Henry here's been through a lot," he added. And then he turned to look at Mikki. "I'll be back in a few minutes. Wait for me?" he asked hopefully.

Truthfully, she didn't want to turn him down, but she felt as if she should. He'd already put himself out a lot today.

Motioning Jeff to the side, she waited until he joined her then asked in a lowered voice, "Don't you want to go straight home after dropping them off?"

"Not particularly. I'm going back to the restaurant. I thought you might want to follow me there for that drink or dessert we talked about," Jeff reminded her.

That had been more than an hour ago, and in all the excitement over Henry's arm, she had honestly forgotten that conversation.

"Are you still up for that?" she asked, surprised.

"More than ever." He grinned, his eyes washing over her. "I have to confess that watching you in action invigorates me."

Mikki's eyes met his. *Right back at you*, she thought. "Okay, I'll wait for you."

"Great," he told her.

He was tempted just to give her a quick kiss on the cheek, but he was afraid that might make her back off or change her mind about waiting for him. He still wasn't sure where he stood, so for now, he was taking baby steps.

He turned toward Mrs. Hendricks and her son. With a flourish, he bowed before the boy and said, "Mrs. Hendricks, your chariot awaits."

"What's a chariot?" Henry asked.

Very gingerly, Jeff picked the boy up. "A stagecoach without a top."

"Your car doesn't have a top?" Henry asked, his eyes widening. "Where is it?"

Jeff looked over toward the boy's mother. "I bet he keeps you on your toes, doesn't he?"

For the first time since she had pounded on the clinic's

door more than an hour ago, Henry's mother smiled as she followed her son and his new hero. "Oh, you have no idea."

Chapter Fourteen

"How did you get to be so good with children?" Mikki asked, sitting across the table from Jeff.

True to his word, Jeff had returned to the clinic less than half an hour after taking Henry and his very relieved mother home. As soon as he had returned, Mikki had locked the facility up again. And then, with his leading the way, she had followed Jeff over to his restaurant.

They were now sitting at a table for two that, unlike the table where they had first shared dinner the other night, was tucked off to one side, away from the other diners.

Because she had liked it so much the last time she'd dined here, Mikki decided to order another slice of tiramisu. Foregoing the wine Jeff had suggested, she'd asked for a glass of sparkling water.

"Well," Jeff answered, "I used to be one myself." When he saw her continue to look at him as if she was waiting for him to elaborate further, he explained, "And I had to look after my brother and sister while my mother was at work. I found that Robert and Tina didn't like having to listen to me, and yelling at them didn't get me anywhere, so I had to come up with a different approach."

A fond smile curved his lips as he recalled those days. Sometimes, it felt like a million years ago. At other times, it was as if it had all happened yesterday.

"I talked to them as if they were human beings— even though—" he laughed "—I had some pretty strong doubts about that at the time."

"Well, your method certainly worked on Henry," Mikki told him. "I don't think I would have been able to get a clear X-ray of his arm, never mind getting that cast on him, without you. Having you there, talking to him, was extremely helpful."

"Glad to be of assistance." Jeff raised his glass in a silent toast to their successful venture. "I did my best."

Taking a sip of wine, he set the glass down again. And then he looked at the woman he found himself growing increasingly attracted to, debating the wisdom of whether or not he should say something. He had a feeling that Mikki would probably prefer that he didn't say anything, but in all good conscience, Jeff really felt that he needed to ask—it had been preying on his mind ever since it happened.

Taking a breath, he pushed on. "You don't do that very often, do you?"

"You mean work late?" Mikki guessed. "About half the time. It's hard turning people away just because they happen to be sitting in the waiting room when it's time to close up."

It was a way out and part of him thought he should take it. But he found that he was worried about her. He didn't want anything happening to her just because she had such a kind heart.

"No," he persisted, "I mean open the doors after hours when everyone else has left the clinic."

Rather than look at the subject in general, Mikki was still focused on the specific. "Mrs. Hendricks was frantic. You saw her."

"I saw her," he agreed. "And I was with you so if there was any danger, I'd be there to protect you." He saw a somewhat skeptical look enter her eyes. Jeff doggedly pressed on. "But what I'm asking about is if you were there alone after hours—if I wasn't there and the nurse was gone—would you open the door?"

Very slowly, her lips curved into a small, touched smile. "Are you worried about me?"

"Guess my secret's out," Jeff quipped, and then he grew serious. "I'm just saying that it's a dangerous neighborhood—it's not like Bedford—and some punk might use a ruse, claiming to be sick, to get into the clinic when no one else is around."

Mikki thought she knew what this was ultimately about—breaking in to steal drugs. "You don't have to worry. All the drugs are securely locked up in the safe," she told him.

How could someone so sharp be so beautifully naive at the same time? "You know the combination?"

"Yes. I have to be able to open the safe in order to dispense the medication," she told him.

He hated having to state the obvious, but maybe if

she heard it, she'd think twice the next time someone was pounding on the doors, asking to be let in after hours. "A desperate punk would think nothing of doing whatever he needed to do to make you open the safe. Or he might not even be after the drugs," Jeff said pointedly, looking at her.

Mikki let out a long breath and inclined her head. "Point taken," she allowed. He wasn't saying anything that hadn't crossed her mind already. "And if it makes you feel any better, that was the first time I was ever alone after hours—and technically," she said, looking at him pointedly, "I really wasn't."

He nodded, but his mind still wasn't at ease. "Promise me that if you ever find yourself in that position again, you'll call me."

Mikki smiled as another forkful of tiramisu disappeared between her lips. "Right. And you'll come running over."

"Yes," he assured her seriously. "I will."

She could have sworn she felt a hot flash passing over her entire body, which was ridiculous because, at thirty-five, she was way too young for that. Mikki admitted to herself that it had more to do with the man sitting across from her than with her age.

"Oh," she finally said, forcing the word out of a mouth that felt bone-dry. She tried not to dwell on him coming to her rescue as if she was some sort of old-fashioned damsel in distress. "Well, lucky for you, I only work there one day a week and this has never happened before, so it shouldn't happen again."

"Yeah, lucky," he repeated in a monotone voice that said he really didn't feel that it was lucky at all. To tell the truth, he rather liked the idea of having to come to her rescue.

Seeing that she had finished both the cake and the goblet of sparkling water, Jeff asked her, "Can I get you anything else?"

"No, thank you." She picked up her purse from the floor next to her, ready to leave. "I think I'd better be getting home. I went in early today and it's been a really long, long day," she emphasized.

"Okay." Jeff rose to his feet. He pulled out her chair for her, then tucked it back up against the table after she stepped away.

When he began to follow her to the door, Mikki paused to tell him, "I know where I left the car this time. You don't have to walk me to the parking lot again."

"I'm not," he answered.

"Then why are you still walking with me?" she asked.

"Because this time," he told her, "I'd like to see you home."

It wasn't as if they were on a date, although she had to admit that maybe, at another time and place, she would have liked that. "There's no need to do that," Mikki told him.

He'd been more than a great help today, starting with all that food he'd brought to the clinic. She didn't want him to feel obligated to do anything more for her.

Then, recalling what he had said earlier about the clinic's location, Mikki reminded him, "After all, this is Bedford."

"I know," he answered amicably, still walking beside her, "but it would just make me feel better to see you to your door."

Well, she wasn't going to argue with him. "I guess chivalry isn't dead," she remarked.

Jeff supposed that was one word for it. But if he were being totally honest, chivalry didn't have anything to do with why he was doing this. He just didn't want the evening to end just yet.

But he had a feeling that if he said as much, that might frighten Mikki away. So he murmured, "I guess not."

Since they had arrived at the restaurant together, their vehicles weren't parked that far apart.

"Wait here," he told her. "I'll get my car and pull up behind you. Then you can lead the way to your house— or apartment," he amended, realizing that he had no idea if she lived in one or the other.

"House," she told him. "It's a house. I live in the Woodbridge development."

That caused him to stop walking for a moment. "You're kidding."

She looked at him, confused. "No, why?"

He laughed. "I live there, too. I guess that kind of makes us neighbors."

Mikki couldn't really explain why she felt that flutter in her stomach when he told her that, or why that flutter seemed to intensify by the moment.

She did her best to appear unaffected. "I guess so," she agreed. "I'm on Mayfair," she told him, then added, "It's a cul-de-sac."

"Alsace," he told her, giving her the name of the street where he lived. "That's on the other side of the development."

She knew that. She knew all the names of the streets in the development. And, considering the size of the neighborhood, his street wasn't all that far away from hers. It probably took ten, maybe twelve minutes to reach on foot.

"Small world," she commented. Belatedly, she noticed that she'd reached her car.

"I was just thinking that," Jeff told her. Pausing for a moment at her car, he nodded. "Okay, I'll go get my car. Be right back."

Her stomach continued to flutter as she watched him go to fetch his vehicle. For a brief moment she told herself that she should go now, while he was getting his car.

But she didn't.

Mikki had no idea why she kept glancing up into her rearview mirror every few minutes. Jeff knew where he was going. It wasn't as if she was going to lose him in the Saturday-night traffic.

It seemed like everyone and his cousin was out on the road tonight, determined to get to wherever a good time could be had. She supposed that she was one of the few people out on the road who just wanted to get home rather than to a club or a party.

The sudden sound of screeching brakes behind her had Mikki automatically tightening her hands on the wheel, instantly alert. Her heart had flown up into her throat and was throbbing hard there.

Straining to see behind her using her side mirror as well as the rearview one, she realized that the screeching sound had come from Jeff's car. He had slammed on his brakes, narrowly avoiding hitting a car that had flown through the intersection and a red light. The driver of the other car just kept going, either unaware or indifferent to the fact that he had nearly been the cause of an accident.

Mikki began to pull over, but she saw that Jeff just kept driving. So she righted her vehicle and continued driving to her house.

But the moment she pulled up in her driveway, less than ten minutes later, she leaped out of her car and quickly ran up to Jeff's vehicle. He was just parking at her front curb.

"Are you all right?" she cried breathlessly.

Getting out, Jeff closed his door. "Well, I'm a little shaken up," he admitted. "But no damage done."

She wasn't as cavalier as he was. "Only because you have quick reflexes. That guy was driving like a maniac. He almost plowed right into you," she said, clearly angry about the incident.

"The main thing was that he *didn't*," Jeff emphasized.

She was stunned that he could take it all in so calmly. "Do you always see the upside like that?"

He was sorry that she'd had to witness the near accident and that it had upset her, but he had his own way of handling things like that, at least when it only involved him.

"That's the only way I can keep things from getting to me. I dwell on the positive." It had been his philosophy in life for as long as he could remember.

Thinking that Mikki probably needed to get some sleep, he was about to say good-night when he took a closer look at her.

Without thinking, he took hold of her shoulders. "Hey, you're shaking. That guy didn't hit your car, did he?" he asked, glancing at the rear of her vehicle. But from what he could see, it was untouched.

"No. But I thought he was going to hit you. *Really* hit you," she stressed. She took a deep breath, steadying her nerves. "Would you like to come in for a drink, or to just pull yourself together?"

She looked like she was the one who needed to be pulled together, not him. He was not about to leave her like this. Dropping his hands to his side, he smiled at her and said, "I thought you didn't drink."

"I'm not on call tonight," Mikki told him. "Someone else is, so I can make an exception this time. Would you like to join me?"

He realized that his heart was not exactly all that steady. Whether that was because of the near accident or because of the invitation, he wasn't sure. But either way, he knew he was going to take her up on it.

"Very much," he replied.

Pointing his key fob toward his car, he pressed the button that brought all four locks down, then turned to follow Mikki to her front door.

"You know, odd as it is to admit," he told her, stopping on her front step, "in all the years I've been driving, that's the first time I ever came close to having someone hit me."

"Have you ever hit anyone—with your car, I mean?" she amended as she unlocked the front door.

"I'm happy to say I never have." And then he grinned. "Do you think that's going to jinx me?"

His question surprised her and she wasn't sure if he was being serious, or just teasing her. "Are you superstitious? Do you believe in jinxes and things like that?"

"No," he answered. "I didn't want to dismiss it out of hand just in case you were superstitious, but no, I don't. I believe in a lot of things, but I don't believe in superstitions."

"What do you believe in?" she asked.

"That's easy," he told her. "I believe in hard work and making your own luck. I believe in treating people the way you want to be treated. I believe in returning favors and sharing whenever possible—and in always taking care of your family and friends."

Mikki looked at him. The man sounded too good to be true. If her mother had come across him, she would already have him bundled up in her car and heading for Las Vegas.

Which was precisely why she was so leery of the feelings that were swirling all through her, Mikki thought. Feelings she had never even briefly entertained before about *anyone*.

Gesturing toward the gray sectional in her living room, she said, "Make yourself comfortable."

Leaving him there, she went into the kitchen and opened the refrigerator. There wasn't all that much to rummage through and definitely not a large selection of alcohol for her to offer him. Actually, there was only one bottle.

"I've got a bottle of rosé," she called out. "Is that all right?"

"Then you do drink," he concluded because up until now, he wasn't sure.

"No," Mikki answered, bringing the bottle and one glass over to him. "My mother does. She brought the rosé over to toast her new engagement."

"Well, then congratulations to your mother," Jeff said.

"No," Mikki corrected. "The wine lasted longer than her engagement. I'm afraid that husband-to-be number five is long gone without ever making it to the altar. But Mother kept the engagement ring—and left me with custody of the wine, which I will now gladly offer to you." She poured part of the contents into the glass she had brought over.

He looked at the lone glass, surprised. "I thought you said you were having some."

"That's right, I did say that, didn't I? Sorry. It's not something I'm used to doing," she confessed. "Let me go get another glass."

Returning from the kitchen, she set the second glass on the coffee table next to his. She only poured half the amount she'd poured for him into her glass, then raised it in a toast. "May you always have near misses."

Jeff raised his own glass. "At least when it comes to car accidents," he amended.

His eyes met hers just before he took a sip.

Chapter Fifteen

Belatedly, because she had been so mesmerized by the look in Jeff's eyes, Mikki came to.

Doing her best to seem nonchalant, she took a sip from her own glass of wine. Less than half a beat late, she could swear that she felt her head beginning to spin.

Granted, she wasn't accustomed to drinking alcohol on anything that even remotely approached a regular basis, but she certainly had had wine before on occasion. And this was rather a light wine at that. She sincerely doubted that the tiny bit she'd just imbibed was responsible for the light-headed feeling she was experiencing right at this moment.

Taking a deep breath, Mikki attempted to distance herself from the thoughts and emotions that were somersaulting through her right now.

She changed the subject. "Um, I've been meaning to

ask you, how is your mother doing? She's almost due for her second recheck," Mikki recalled.

After the seemingly nonstop day Mikki had just had, he appreciated her being so thoughtful and asking about his mother. The woman really was one of a kind.

"She's doing well. She's also thinking of adopting you," he confided.

"Excuse me?"

Jeff backtracked, starting from the beginning. "To be honest, she's surprised that she's feeling so well. I'm only just now beginning to find out that she'd been hiding just how bad she'd been feeling all this time. But now that she's feeling better, she's finally admitting the true extent of her pain."

He paused, letting that sink in, then said, "Since you, in effect, made it all better, my mother wants to show her gratitude. Best way she knows how is to adopt you."

Mikki laughed. "Tell your mother I'm very happy I could help her and I'm touched that she wants to make me part of her family, but I really don't need to be adopted. I have a mother." She paused as she took another long sip of her wine, nearly finishing what had been a very small amount to begin with. "I have to admit that she's more like a character out of a play, but I have a mother," she told him.

There was a lot of history behind that one sentence, Jeff guessed. He could hear it in her intonation. She had aroused his curiosity. "Tell me about her."

Mikki shook her head, dismissing the request. "You don't want to hear about my mother."

"Sure I do," he told her, sitting up. "She sounds colorful."

Mikki considered his comment. "That would be one word for her."

"What would be another?" he asked.

Other than confiding in Nikki, she had decided a long time ago to keep her mother's misdeeds and the way she felt about them to herself.

The glass was empty and she twirled the stem between her thumb and forefinger, searching for a way to frame her answer—or a way to deflect.

"Although neither one of my parents actually taught me this by word or example, I really, truly believe that if you can't say something nice about a person, you shouldn't say anything at all."

He read between the lines. "That bad, huh?"

Mikki shrugged. Why did she feel this overwhelming desire to share any of this with this man? It wasn't that her mother deserved her loyalty—if the tables were reversed, her mother certainly wouldn't keep any less than stellar details about her private. But Mikki just didn't believe in airing her dirty laundry in public.

"My mother has her demons," Mikki said tactfully. And then, because this wasn't exactly a secret, she said, "She's an insecure woman who is actively searching for a Prince Charming to simultaneously sweep her off her feet and worship the ground she walks on."

He raised his eyebrows, clearly trying to picture what she'd just described. "Sounds like that's a tall order."

"It's an impossible order," Mikki corrected.

Her childhood must have been hell, Jeff thought. With that in mind, there were a thousand ways her life could have gone awry. "Well, even so, it looks like you turned out all right."

An ironic smile curved her lips. "That was more in

self-defense than anything else," she told him. "Rather than spending my time getting all bogged down frantically trying to find happiness, I thought it was more important to try to get outside myself and help others."

There was a little wine left in his glass, and he raised it in another toast to her. "Well, on behalf of those others, I'd like to thank you for that."

She didn't like having attention focused on her. That was her mother's thing, not hers. "You're not exactly a slouch in that department," she countered. "You can't tell me that you always drive around with that much food in your car."

"Oh." Now he understood what Mikki was talking about. "That."

"Yes, that," Mikki laughed. She liked the fact that he was modest and didn't brag. She found it really refreshing, especially after having grown up in her parents' world.

"Well, I never got to be a Boy Scout, but I do believe in always being prepared," Jeff told her.

"For what?" she asked. "An impromptu banquet? Admit it, you brought all that food with you because you knew I wouldn't leave my patients to have lunch while they were stuck in the waiting room, hungry." Which, in her book, meant that he'd been paying close attention to the way she thought and behaved.

"I guess I'm guilty as charged," Jeff allowed vaguely.

"You're a very generous man, Jeff Sabatino," she told him.

"Maybe you bring out the best in me," he suggested.

He was sitting right next to her on the sectional. Because her hair was falling into her face, he gently moved it aside with the tip of his fingers. He wanted to get a better look into her eyes.

There went her stomach again, Mikki thought, feeling it do a somersault.

Breathe, damn it, breathe!

"I don't think it needs to be brought out," she told him, her voice sounding strangely low to her own ear. It was as if the words were struggling to emerge. "I think it's right there on the surface."

"Careful," he told her, his voice as low as hers. He set his empty glass down on the coffee table. "You'll turn my head."

It was as if everything around her had fallen into darkness. All she was aware of was him. "I wouldn't want to do that," she answered.

"I totally agree," he whispered. "Because then I might miss."

She didn't have to ask him what he meant by that, or what he'd miss, because the next moment Jeff went on to show her.

He lowered his mouth to hers.

Oh, no!

The words echoed in her brain in giant capital letters. This was worse than she thought.

She was really hoping that his kiss would be anticlimactic. That it would leave her cold and she could return to her isolated little world, none the worse for the experience.

But his kiss *wasn't* anticlimactic. It was, in a word, *delicious*. Delicious and it left her wanting more. So much so that she slid into not just the kiss, but somehow into him, as well.

Whatever space had been between them on the sectional was gone. Gone to the point that not even a well-worn dime could be wedged between them.

Everything she had hoped not to feel she was, in essence, feeling. Heat and desire, and everything inside her was churning and swirling.

He hadn't counted on this.

All he had wanted to do was kiss a beautiful woman—maybe several times—and then take his leave before desire had an opportunity to intensify, making him want to stay.

But desire had immediately taken on depth and breadth from the first moment of contact.

Jeff didn't remember enfolding her in his arms, didn't remember deepening the kiss until it was completely fathomless. Just like that, he was lost in an ocean of heated emotions.

He found himself not just wanting to kiss her, but wanting to make love with her.

Now.

And although he didn't detect so much as even mild resistance on her part, he wasn't about to overwhelm her in any manner, shape or form. It wouldn't be right.

And more than that, it was no way to repay her for what she'd done for his mother and, thus, for him. She had performed a selfless act and he was behaving, in a word, selfishly.

But he couldn't.

Exercising more strength and self-control than he'd ever had the need to before, Jeff ended the kiss and then drew away from this woman who lit him up.

There was a look of surprise on Mikki's upturned

face. Surprise and more than a little confusion. Her eyes were wide as she looked at him.

"I should go home," he told her, stringing the words together with effort.

She wasn't sure what Jeff was actually telling her. Was he rejecting her, or had he changed his mind? In either case, she went along with it.

"I guess it's my turn to walk you to the door," she said with a smile, congratulating herself that her voice didn't crack.

"You don't have to do that," he replied, trying to keep the situation light. "The door's not that hard to find."

"I have to lock it when you leave," she pointed out.

"Oh, right." He felt awkward about the whole situation. About giving in to his desires, and then about having to stop. "All right then," Jeff said, gathering himself together.

He had to admit that he was rather surprised at the impact she'd just had on him. The woman was absolutely intoxicating, far more than the wine he'd just had. Even more than straight whiskey. Yes, she was beautiful, but in no way had he been prepared for her having such a lethal mouth.

"Let's go," he said, leading the way to her front door. He reached it in several steps. Turning around to face her, he said, "Well, we're here."

"Yes," Mikki answered, her heart hammering wildly as she contemplated her next move, "I guess we are."

He was about to say something further, but he didn't get the chance. Because the very next moment, instead of saying "Goodbye," Mikki was saying "Hello" in the most basic way possible.

Almost on automatic pilot for the very first time in

her life, Mikki had threaded her arms around his neck and raised herself up on her toes until her mouth was less than a breath away from his.

And then it wasn't away at all.

It was hard to say, when she tried to analyze it later, who had moved in first. Whether she had completed the move or if he had beaten her to it.

Either way, it didn't matter who was first.

All that mattered was that when contact was finally made, fireworks went off, sealing them to one another and guaranteeing that they would remain that way, at least for the time being.

He had both wanted this, and he hadn't. Wanted it because the very feel of her breath aroused him to such heights, it caused him to become instantly dizzy, instantly hungry.

But he didn't want her to feel that this was because he had come to the clinic today. Didn't want her thinking that this was his endgame and once he reached it, the game would be over.

Because whatever was happening right now, it was far from over. And while he couldn't be accused of being a saint, or even remotely close to one, none of the women he had been with and enjoyed had ever caused this extreme, instant reaction within him.

He could barely contain himself.

And he didn't want to.

What he wanted was to make love to every single part of her—simultaneously. Wanted it so much, it nearly scared the hell out of him.

This was something completely brand-new, and he had no idea how to react to it.

* * *

She shouldn't be letting this happen, Mikki thought. Shouldn't be letting it happen because the firm ground she'd thought she was standing on had vanished underneath her.

And the worst part of it was that she didn't care.

The only thing she cared about was that she didn't want whatever this was to stop.

Ever.

The only kind of hunger she had ever known was the kind that was satisfied by food. But this hunger was something entirely new, entirely different. She could honestly say that it was frightening in its insatiability.

Since they had come together at her door under the guise of saying goodbye, she hadn't even stopped for air. All she wanted was to feel his hands along her body, his lips devouring hers before they ultimately moved on to leave their imprint along every throbbing inch of her skin.

Between the door and the sectional, clothes wound up vanishing, both his and hers—Mikki really didn't remember how and when. When they were on the sectional, she was only aware of the heat radiating from her body, heat mingling with his.

Their bodies tangled together, and it was as if they were both bent on mutual pleasure while bringing one another up to heights that caused mountains to look small by comparison.

Mikki didn't want to feel this way, didn't want to feel as if she could touch the very sky. Because that meant that the eventual *lack* of this exhilarating feeling would bring with it an inconceivable pain. It would consume her and then spit her out. In pieces.

She didn't want to become like her mother—not even close.

And yet, she couldn't help herself. Couldn't stop reacting to Jeff. Couldn't stop these passions, these longings, from taking hold of her and keeping her imprisoned in their grip.

All right, all right, if this was her fate, Mikki decided, then she was going to make the most of it. And when it was gone, when *he* had gone on with his life and left hers, she'd force herself to accept it.

But right now, it wasn't gone. *He* wasn't gone. He was here, bringing her to the very brink of explosions time and again.

Unable to catch her breath, she was determined not to be the only one to remember this night for years to come. So for every sensation Jeff created within her, she reciprocated, mimicking his moves and then, going on instinct, creating some of her own. Each time his hands passed over her, caressing her, stimulating her, she did the same to him.

When she heard him moan, she knew she was succeeding and that spurred her on.

The woman was a veritable wildcat.

He'd had no idea that she was capable of this. Talk about still waters running deep—Mikki was an ocean. What he had discovered about her was utterly mindblowing.

To think he had been worried about taking advantage of her. Hell, he could barely keep up.

With what amounted to the last of his strength, Jeff sealed his mouth to hers after reanointing every part of her body with that same mouth. And then, bringing himself up along the length of her, he united their two bodies.

An urgency mounted within him even though he managed to go slowly at first. That quickly evaporated as she moved beneath him, fanning his desires. Making him go faster and faster.

He seized the moment, driving her up further. He felt her nails digging into his back, heard her breathing growing more and more rapid. When she arched against him, uttering a muffled cry, he knew that they had reached the ultimate peak together.

When the explosion came, he clung to her and the moment, his heart pounding as hard as hers was. He could feel it against his chest. It blended with the sensation of the incredible rush that was passing over him, enfolding them both.

And though it seemed impossible, at that moment, he knew he was in love with her.

Chapter Sixteen

"That was incredible," Jeff whispered. His breath ruffled her hair as Mikki lay with her head on his chest. "I have to admit, you turned out to be a complete surprise."

Mikki raised her head and looked at him. "Why? What were you expecting?"

"Well—" he laughed softly, running his hand along her back, caressing her skin "—certainly not to have my shoes and socks blown off."

"What shoes and socks? You were naked," she pointed out with a grin.

"All the harder to do," he replied, then laughed again. "I just want you to know that I had absolutely no intentions of that happening when I came over here tonight."

"Are you apologizing or telling me that you're having regrets?" Mikki asked him, drawing away and wondering just how she was going to execute a retreat at this point without feeling like a complete idiot.

"Neither," he answered, tightening his arm around her. "I just want you to know that I didn't have any ulterior motives coming over." Jeff played with the ends of her hair as he talked. "To be honest, I guess I was kind of in awe, watching you in action today, especially when you were with Henry. You're really something, you know that?"

She shifted slightly, feeling somewhat self-conscious. Compliments had that effect on her. Especially in this situation. "You don't have to say things like that after the fact."

"After what fact?" Jeff asked her. With his forefinger, he raised her chin so he could look into her eyes.

"You know." When he continued to look at her, obviously waiting for her to go on, she forced herself to explain. "I'm saying we've already made love—you don't have to try to soften me up."

Mystified, he told her, "I'm not trying to soften you up. I'm just telling you what I'm feeling right now. Just what kind of men have you been out with?"

"None," she answered. And then, shrugging, she added, "Not in a very long, long time."

"Then where's this coming from?" he asked, wanting to know why she seemed so insecure. If anyone had a reason to be confident, it was Mikki. "A bad experience?"

She thought back to her first—and only—experience with a man. She'd been a sophomore in college and he was a TA. "Maybe," she admitted. "A very long time ago. More like a mistake, really."

Even though Jeff had a lot of questions he wanted to ask her, he knew it wasn't his place to pry.

"Well," Jeff began slowly, his voice soft, low and deliberately soothing, "I don't know how you feel about what just happened, but for me, it definitely wasn't a mistake." Ever so lightly, he ran the back of his hand along her cheek, stirring her. Stirring himself. "On the contrary, it was as close to heaven as I've ever been."

"Are you trying to seduce me?" Mikki asked incredulously.

His mouth curved in a teasing smile. "Maybe. How'm I doing?" he asked.

"Keep going," Mikki encouraged him. "I'll let you know."

"Nothing I like better than a challenge," Jeff told her, leaning over Mikki just before he brought his mouth down to hers.

It was just at that very heated, intimate moment that the phone suddenly rang. It was the landline rather than her cell phone, and the shrill sound shattered the air as it wedged its way into what was the beginning of another beautifully romantic interlude.

Jeff drew back. He looked at the landline accusingly. "Can you ignore that?"

Mikki sighed. "No."

He moved aside, resigned, as he allowed Mikki to sit up so that she could get to the telephone. "I didn't think so."

Reaching for the receiver, Mikki picked it up and brought it to her ear. "Hello, this is Dr. McKenna."

As he watched, Mikki transformed from the desirable woman he was about to make love with for a second time to the very efficient doctor he'd seen in action earlier at the clinic.

Mikki listened in silence, then said, "Yes, of course, I'll be there as soon as I can. Watch his vitals," she instructed the person on the other end of the line just before she hung up. She looked at Jeff. "I have to go."

"I kind of figured that out," he said wryly. And then he remembered something. "I thought you had someone covering for you."

"I do. But this is an extenuating circumstance," she explained, getting up from the sectional. She saw that Jeff was waiting for an explanation. "I operated on this man a little over a week ago. He was discharged."

"What went wrong?" he asked as they both began picking their clothes up from the floor and getting dressed.

Jeff could tell by her voice was she was trying not to sound irritated. "My patient decided he didn't have to take it easy for a few weeks the way I told him to. He was in his garage, trying to fix something, when he tripped over a box of tools and fell. He ripped open some of his stitches, and his wife panicked and drove him to the ER. He asked for me, telling the doctor on duty that he wouldn't let anyone else touch him."

Mikki sighed as she pulled up the zipper on her jeans. Finished dressing, she looked at Jeff, disappointment suddenly welling up within her. "I'm sorry."

"For what?" Jeff asked. "For being you? Hey, I understand." He knew exactly what he had signed on for when he had begun thinking of her in a romantic light. She was a doctor, and this came with the package. "I have a feeling that my mother probably feels the same way about you that this guy in the ER does." Jeff put his shoes on and stood up again. "Want me to drive you to the hospital?"

"That's really nice of you to offer," Mikki answered, "but you should go home. At least one of us should get some rest. Besides," she added, "until I see the amount of damage he's done to himself, I have no idea how long this is going to take."

"And no one else can sub for you?" Jeff asked in one last-ditch attempt to prolong their evening.

"If I was incapacitated or unreachable, they could probably come up with someone. But a doctor-patient relationship is really important to me, and it takes time to build up. Since he specifically asked for me, I wouldn't feel right about letting my patient down."

Jeff nodded, making his peace with the situation. "I guess I should just be glad that the hospital didn't call any sooner." Leaning over, he lightly brushed his lips over hers. "Sure I can't drive you?"

"I'm sure—but I really do appreciate the offer." She realized that she was guilty of rushing him out. She didn't want to come across that way, not after the wonderful evening she'd just had with him. "You can stay here if you like."

But Jeff shook his head. "I'm afraid that it just wouldn't be the same without you."

He stood there, waiting for her to get her purse. When she was ready, he walked out with her and waited as she locked her front door. "I'll call you," he told her.

Mikki nodded, telling herself not to cling to that. It wasn't a promise. It was just something guys said after an evening was over, even a wonderful evening. If she held him to that and he didn't call, she ran the risk of being crushed, just like her mother.

Besides, Mikki reminded herself as she drove to the hospital, *you don't believe in commitment, or happily-ever-afters, remember?*

As far as happily-ever-after went, she had absolutely

nothing to base it on or refer to as an example. None of her mother's marriages had lasted. Not to mention that Veronica certainly hadn't been happy during those marriages' short lifespans.

Maybe this was all for the best, Mikki told herself. One really fantastic night and now she was going back to life as she knew it, doing what she was really good at and was meant to do: be a doctor.

She forced herself to loosen her death grip on the steering wheel as she drove into the hospital's parking lot.

Mikki found it difficult to refrain from being curt when she spoke to Mr. Miller, the returning gallstone patient who had inadvertently cut her evening short. She wanted to lecture him, not just because of her shortened evening, but because the man had wantonly ignored her instructions.

The repercussions for that could have been very serious. Luckily, they weren't.

However, she found that it was difficult to be angry with her patient when he appeared so utterly relieved to see her.

"You were supposed to take it easy, Mr. Miller," she told him as she pulled on a pair of rubber gloves.

Drawing back his hospital gown, she closely examined the extent of repair that needed to be done.

Miller, a heavyset man in his sixties, shifted uncomfortably at the admonishment. "I didn't mean to trip over that toolbox and fall down," he said, as if that absolved him of his part in this.

Mikki raised her eyes to his for a moment. "I'm sure you didn't," she answered.

Miller's wife cut in. "I *told* him not to go into that garage. I *told* him to sit in his recliner and watch that

movie with me, but would he listen?" Mrs. Miller lamented. "No, he had to go try to fix the heating unit.
Said he needed to feel 'useful.'" Mrs. Miller laughed
harshly. "I ask you, what do you do with a man like
that?"

Mikki could see how uncomfortable her patient was
becoming as his wife harped on his less than sensible
behavior. She smiled at the man before answering his
wife's question.

"Just love him, I guess. And stitch him up," Mikki
added. Finished with her preliminary exam, she told her
patient, "You didn't do as much damage as you thought.
You do need some stitches. But I need to clean this up
first," she said, nodding at the broken stitches and the
dried blood around them.

"I don't have to stay here overnight, do I?" Miller
asked, concerned.

"What, you don't like our accommodations?" she
asked, doing her best to look serious.

"It's not that," her patient assured her quickly. "I just
want to go home."

She could understand that, Mikki thought. Who
wanted to stay overnight in a hospital? "I think we can
arrange that. Wait here while I have the nurse get a
fresh suture kit."

Although everything went off without a hitch, it was
close to three o'clock before Mikki walked back through
her front door again.

The first thing that struck her was that the house
felt oddly empty, even though there was never anyone
else here when she got home. She didn't even have a
pet dog or cat, or a parakeet, to chase away the silence.

Given that, why the emptiness seemed to seep into her this way tonight didn't make any sense.

Because she felt so drained, Mikki paused to sit down on the sectional to kick off her shoes.

She knew she was probably imagining things, but she could have sworn that she detected the scent of Jeff's aftershave lotion. She was undoubtedly just punchy. Even so, she leaned over the cushion and took a deep breath.

And then she smiled.

It *wasn't* her imagination, she thought. Picking up the cushion, she held it for a moment and took in another deep breath. It smelled just like Jeff. She could even feel things stirring within her.

C'mon, get a grip. You're a respected physician surgeon, not a twelve-year-old with her first crush.

She was acting like some kind of an adolescent, Mikki upbraided herself. Worse than that, she was behaving like her mother every time her mother had been on the brink of yet another "love of her life" adventure. An adventure that always seemed to turn out to be another huge disappointment.

Well, she wasn't her mother and she didn't need or want that, Mikki silently insisted, tossing the cushion back where it belonged.

Come Monday morning, she would have the cushions dry-cleaned, she promised herself. As for now, she was going to go to bed and sleep—maybe even until Monday morning.

The idea heartened her.

Getting up from the sectional, she was about to head for the stairs and her bedroom when she saw a flashing light out of the corner of her eye. It caught her attention.

It was the light on her landline—someone had left a message while she was at the hospital.

Her first thought was that the hospital had called again, alerting her about another patient. But then, she decided, someone would have undoubtedly said something while she was there.

Reevaluating the situation, she sincerely doubted that the message on her answering machine had anything to do with Mr. Miller and his stitches.

Maybe it was her mother, calling to tell her "wonderful news, darling!" which was the way all Veronica's announcements about a new man in her life started out.

Well, if that was it, it could wait until morning, Mikki thought. She wasn't in the mood to try to humor her mother.

The next moment she realized that the message on her phone couldn't have been from her mother. While the woman still stayed up until all hours of the night, she had never known her mother to call after midnight.

"Stop guessing, idiot, and play the message," she ordered herself. "Maybe, if you're lucky, it's a wrong number or some prince, offering to leave his entire fortune to you—all you need to go is send him a cashier's check for a nominal sum and the rest will all be yours."

Lord, she was beyond punchy. Sitting down on the sectional again, she pulled the phone over to her and pressed the play button.

At first, all she heard was jarring static, followed by a spat of nothing. And the metallic voice on the machine informed her in a formal tone that was the end of the message.

As she started to push the phone back to its original position on the side table, she heard the answering machine go through the motions of queuing up a second call.

There had been two of them?

As she stared at the device, a second message came on.

"Sorry, that last call was me. I hung up because I didn't want you to get the idea that I was, well, stalking you."

Mikki straightened, at attention and hardly breathing.

That was Jeff's voice.

"But I really want to know that you got back safe. I know, I know, you've been doing this forever, but well… I just want to make sure you got in all right. Am I being out of line? Yeah, probably, but in my defense, I'm my mother's son and there's this recessive gene she passed on to my siblings and me. It's called the worry gene, and sometimes it kicks into high gear. When it does, the idea of getting any sleep goes right out the window.

"I'm rambling," he apologized. "Ignore what I just said. Except for this part: I had a really great time tonight—or more accurately, I guess, *last* night. I just wanted you to know that. Hope everything turned out okay with your patient—how can it not, right? You're his doctor.

"I'd better hang up now before I put my other foot into my mouth or say something even more stupid. Oh, and this isn't what I meant when I said I'd call you. It just happened." He sounded as if he was uncomfortable with the way he had to be coming across and cleared his throat. "Good night, Mikki. I hope that you managed to get some sleep."

The dial tone followed after the message ended. And

then the metallic voice informed her that there were no more messages.

Mikki smiled to herself as she looked at the now silent answering machine.

She changed her mind about going up to her bedroom. Instead, she curled up on the sectional and pulled the cushion closer to her.

She rested her cheek against it.

In a few minutes, she'd fallen asleep that way.

Chapter Seventeen

It was a first.

Ordinarily, she was a very light sleeper. But the sound of ringing slowly registered in Mikki's head in small increments. When she first became aware of it, she thought it was just part of her dream.

Eventually, she realized that it wasn't and she reached for the telephone on the side table next to the sectional. It was only when she heard the dial tone against her ear while the ringing continued that she realized it wasn't her phone.

Someone was ringing her doorbell.

Mikki was on her feet before she managed to completely banish the fog from her brain. Maybe she was getting old, she thought, struggling to focus. There was a time when she could go almost two days straight without any sleep and still function.

As she made her way to the front door, Mikki dragged one hand through her hair in a semiattempt to somehow neaten it a little.

Reaching the door, she looked through the peephole—and then blinked to make sure that her eyes weren't playing tricks on her.

Stunned, she didn't open the door immediately. "Jeff? What are you doing here?"

"Right now, standing on your doorstep with groceries that are getting progressively heavier." He shifted the bags to get a better grip. "Mind if I come in?"

Rather than answer his question verbally, Mikki unlocked the door, opened it and stepped back so he could enter.

"Thanks." Shifting the bags again, Jeff walked in.

"I'm sorry, did we talk about this and I forgot?" she asked, confused.

Jeff headed straight for her kitchen. "No, but I thought you might be hungry after going back to the hospital last night. Don't forget, I got a glimpse of the inside of your refrigerator. There was nothing in it except for that bottle of rosé.

"I can't stay long," he told her, unpacking the four bags of groceries he'd brought in, haphazardly placing the items on the kitchen table before organizing the contents according to type. "I've got to be at the restaurant early today, but I thought I'd make you breakfast before I went."

When he turned around to look at her, he saw the expression on her face. Mikki didn't appear to be upset, but she did look rather conflicted. "Did I do something wrong?" Jeff asked.

"No," she answered a bit too quickly. "No, you

didn't." What was wrong with her? She should be happy that he was being so nice. "You're being kind, and caring and, in a word, *terrific*." She paused, running her tongue along her lips, searching for the right words. "And that's just the problem."

He was doing his best to understand what she was trying to tell him. "I can scowl while I'm making breakfast," he offered. "Better yet, I could burn the toast. Would that help?"

He must think she was crazy. Not that anyone would blame him. She tried again.

"I'm sorry. It's just that this whole thing is wonderful and I know what happens when things are wonderful."

Jeff waited for her to continue. She was obviously having trouble expressing what was bothering her. He couldn't pretend to understand, but after last night, he was certainly more than willing to try.

"I'm listening," he told her. It was getting late and he didn't have all that much time. "Would you mind if I put the groceries away while I listened?" he asked, not wanting her to think that he wasn't paying attention to her, or that he was just humoring her by saying he was listening while he was doing something else.

"You probably think I'm crazy," she told him, at a loss as to how to explain any of this to a man for whom most women would kill to have in her life.

"No," Jeff answered patiently. "I think that maybe you're having ambivalent feelings. And I'm probably contributing to that by coming on so strong. I have a habit of doing that when I feel so keenly about something."

He didn't want to crowd her or risk losing her because she felt smothered. He wanted her to take all the time in the world—as long as she eventually came up with the right answer.

"Look, why don't I just make you breakfast and then go so you can eat in peace?" he suggested.

"No," Mikki protested. This wasn't turning out right.

Jeff opened one cabinet after another, looking for a couple of frying pans. "You want to eat in chaos?" he deadpanned.

"I don't want to chase you away—" she protested. However, he deserved to hear the truth. "But I don't want to fall in love with you, either."

Finding the pans, he almost dropped them before he finally put them on the stove. *Was* she falling in love with him? He tried not to react to that and instead said, "Mind if I ask why?"

"Because if I fall in love with you," she said in despair, "it's all going to fall apart."

He glanced at her over his shoulder. It was really getting hard trying to keep the conversation light. But he was determined not to frighten her off and to get to the bottom of what she was trying to tell him. "You read the fine print?"

"Stop making jokes," Mikki lamented. "I'm being serious."

"That's why I'm making jokes," he told her. "Because that's my way of coping with something I don't understand." He sighed as he rolled the matter over in his head. In a way, he kind of understood what she was trying to say. "Okay, how about this. I'll make breakfast, then you eat that breakfast while I go to my restaurant to catch up on some things and also get the place ready for the Strausses' fiftieth wedding anniversary party. And after I'm finished—and you're finished—we'll take things as slow as you want. How's that?"

"You're willing to do that?" she asked, surprised. She'd been afraid that she'd ruined everything.

"Yes. I'm willing to do whatever you ask—as long as you don't ask me to walk away. Not from the best person I've found in a very, very long time."

She took a long breath, feeling like someone who had come perilously close to falling over the brink—and then stepped back.

"I need to explain something to you," she said.

"No, you don't," he told her. "You don't have to explain anything."

"Yes, I do," she countered.

He heard the almost desperate note in her voice and that made him change direction. "Okay then, I'm listening. But I really do have to leave soon, so I'm going to be making your breakfast while I'm listening."

Mikki laughed, shaking her head. "You really are something else."

"And I hope to prove that to you—slowly," Jeff added, mindful of what he'd just promised her a few minutes ago. "Go ahead," he urged as he began to whip up a ham-and-cheese omelet along with a serving of French toast.

She wasn't proud of what she was about to share, but he needed to understand why she was so leery of having a relationship. She knew she'd already touched on this, but he had to be made to understand the full extent of how much this had affected her.

"When I was a kid, I thought everybody's parents argued all the time because mine did. But despite the arguments—and there were some knock-down, drag-out ones—we were a family and I thought we'd always stay that way. But we didn't."

Afraid of seeing pity in his eyes, she stared at the napkin holder in the center of the kitchen table.

"My parents got divorced before I was twelve. My mother fell wildly in love with Albert. They were married before her divorce papers were dry. I didn't realize it then, but that was the start of a pattern.

"My mother would fall head over heels for some 'absolutely wonderful guy,' and they'd get married, but before too long, Mr. Wonderful would stop being wonderful and just become another albatross around her neck. An albatross she'd shed the moment she found her next Mr. Wonderful."

She'd mentioned some of this before, but he hadn't realized the extent of it, or how much it had traumatized her, Jeff thought. "How many times has your mother been married?"

"Four," Mikki answered, then corrected herself. "Five if you count the annulment."

He put the diced bits of ham and cheese into the egg mixture, whisking everything together. "Annulment?"

She nodded. "Harvey," she said. "I'm not sure about the circumstances. I was in medical school at the time. All I know was that by the time I received her announcement saying she'd married Harvey Winthrop, Mother was already getting the union annulled." Mikki sighed. "From that point on, I learned not to ask any questions," she confessed. "It was a lot less stressful that way."

She paused, allowing the import of her words to sink in. "What I'm saying is that my mother taught me by her example that nothing ever lasts, no matter how fantastic it might seem at the outset."

The omelet was ready. He slid it onto a plate, then placed it on the table in front of her. He set the slice of French toast he'd prepared at the same time right next to it.

Clearing off the counter, Jeff picked his words carefully, not wanting to scare her or make her think that he was making light of what she had gone through. "From what you just told me, I can see why you'd feel so leery about entering any sort of a relationship. But I'd like the opportunity to prove to you—slowly," he underscored, "that it doesn't have to be that way.

"But right now," he went on, drying his hands on one of the kitchen towels, "I've got to go and start preparations for that fiftieth wedding anniversary celebration. That's fifty years," he emphasized, his eyes meeting hers. "With the same person." Having made her breakfast and having said what he'd come to say, Jeff paused to kiss her quickly. "It happens more often than you think."

When she rose from the table, he looked at her. "Where are you going?"

She gestured in the general direction of the front door. "I thought I'd see you out."

"Eat the omelet," he told her. "It tastes better warm than cold." He winked at her. "I'll call you."

Mikki sank back down in the chair. After a minute, she began to eat the omelet and French toast he had made for her. While she ate, she wondered if she had just managed to ruin the best thing that had happened to her—or if she had just carried out a preemptive strike, saving herself from experiencing devastating heartache in the near future.

Jeff didn't call.

Not that afternoon and not that evening. When he didn't call the next morning, she tried to tell herself that he was busy. Busy with the restaurant, busy with the party, both before and after, and busy with life in general.

And since it was now Monday, her own routine began all over again, a routine that kept her almost too busy to breathe. And almost too busy to think.

Almost.

Every time her phone rang, whether the landline or her cell, she expected it to be Jeff on the other end.

And when it wasn't, she upbraided herself for thinking—hoping—that it was.

Obviously she'd been right to put the brakes on, Mikki thought, struggling to keep the hurt at bay. She would have felt that much worse if this happened in the future, after she'd invested a lot of time in Jeff. Time and emotions.

Right, like you didn't do any of that already, she mocked herself.

When her phone rang as she walked in her front door at the end of the next day, Mikki flew across the room and grabbed the landline receiver with both hands, simultaneously praying that the person on the other end was Jeff.

But it wasn't.

It was her mother. She'd been in such a hurry to answer the phone, she hadn't bothered to look at the caller

ID. She was slipping again, but then, she supposed she could be forgiven. She was still dealing with the fact that when Sophia Sabatino had come in for her second postsurgical exam, her daughter, Tina, had come with her.

Mikki had expected to see Jeff.

It was over, she thought. Over before it actually began.

Her mother's voice jarred her back to the present.

"Sweetheart, I wanted to you be the first to know," her mother gushed in that familiar voice she knew all too well. "I'm getting married."

Mikki pressed her lips together to suppress the sigh that had instantly risen in response to her mother's news. She was supposed to feign happiness, then ask about the groom-to-be and wish her mother well. But she just couldn't do that. Not again.

So instead of dutifully playing her part, Mikki sank down on the sectional and braced herself. "Why?"

Instead of being annoyed by the challenge the way Mikki had expected her to be, Veronica giggled.

"Well, it's not because I have to, not in *that* way," she heard her mother laugh, "if that's what you're asking me."

Her mother was well past childbearing age no matter how many times she fudged the date on her birth certificate. They both knew that.

"No, Mother, I'm asking why are you going through all this again?"

"Why, because I love Randolph, that's why," her mother answered, sounding surprised that she was even being asked such a question. "It's what people do when they're in love, darling. They get married."

Mikki closed her eyes, searching for strength. "Mother, you have been in love with enough men to form a small army—and each of those men has turned out not to be the soul mate that you thought they were."

Undaunted, her mother said, "I know that, but Randolph—"

This time, she wasn't going to back away. This time she was determined to talk some sense into her mother. She needed to stop this insane cycle of fall in love, marry, divorce, repeat.

"—is probably going to wind up disappointing you, too," Mikki pointed out.

"What would make you say such a thing?" her mother asked, sounding shocked and appalled.

Mikki dug in. Her mother's recurring pattern of behavior was what was responsible for destroying her optimism. She needed to make her mother change. "Because I'm tired of watching you be disappointed time after time."

Her mother was quiet for a moment and Mikki thought that, finally confronted with the truth, maybe her mother had just hung up on her.

But then she heard her mother's voice. "That's very sweet of you, dear," she said patiently. "But I think you're missing the point."

This was where the double-talk came in. This was where her mother started building castles in the sky.

She felt as if she was banging her head against a brick wall.

"And what is the point, Mother?" she asked.

"That's really very simple, dear," her mother said, talking to her as if Mikki were just becoming an adult. "The point is that if I don't go out and seize the moment, if I don't believe that this next union will be the right one and the man that I'm exchanging vows with is going to be the one destined to be by my side for the rest of my life, well, then I might as well just give up on life entirely.

"You have to understand that things don't happen if you sit the game out on the sidelines, Michelle. Things only happen if you have enough courage to go out there and fight for your happiness. *Really* fight for it. If you don't try, you don't win. Do you understand what I'm telling you, Michelle?"

Yes. You're spouting every single cliché out there, Mikki thought, feeling like she was engaged in a losing battle.

But she also remembered reading somewhere that clichés only existed because, at the bottom, they were rooted in the truth.

Besides, maybe her mother was right. Maybe *this* man was going to turn out to be the right one for her. Who was she to say no?

"Yes, Mother," Mikki answered. "Where there's life, there's hope."

"Exactly!" her mother exclaimed. "You *do* understand! So you'll come to the wedding?"

"I'll come to the wedding," Mikki promised.

"Wonderful!" her mother cried. "I can't wait for you to meet Randolph—your new stepfather."

Oh, Lord, Mikki thought, closing her eyes as she searched for strength.

Chapter Eighteen

Mikki felt as if she couldn't find a place for herself. Tension resulting from the last few days, especially after she'd weathered the disappointment of not having Jeff accompanying his mother for her second postsurgical exam, was beginning to tie her up in knots.

With all that going on, who would have thought that her mother could actually say something sensible?

Maybe she should be looking out her window, waiting for the arrival of the four horsemen, Mikki thought, because obviously the end of the world was coming.

She was happy for her mother, happy that her mother felt that she had finally found the right man. Chances of that proving true were slim, but if Veronica could still believe in miracles, why shouldn't she?

But meanwhile, her own life suddenly looked as if it was in complete disarray and she had no idea how to fix it, or even if it *was* fixable.

Maybe she should call Jeff.

Or maybe she shouldn't, because the two of them just weren't meant to be.

When the phone rang again a little more than five minutes later, she looked at the landline accusingly. "Give me a break, Mother," she muttered under her breath.

It rang again and she knew her mother wouldn't stop calling until she answered.

Crossing back to the landline, she yanked the receiver from its cradle.

"I said I'll come." It was an effort not to snap the words out. After all, what she was going through really wasn't her mother's fault. This was all her own doing.

"I haven't asked yet," the deep voice on the other end said, "but good to know."

The receiver almost slid out of her hand. Was she getting a do-over? "Jeff?"

"I take it that response when you picked up the phone wasn't meant for me."

Relief at hearing his voice temporarily made her mind go blank. It took Mikki a second to pull herself together and answer him. "I thought you were my mother, calling back."

"Oh, if you're expecting her call, I'll just hang up," Jeff offered.

"No!" she cried. If he hung up, he might never call back again. And then she realized how desperate that plea had to have sounded to him. Embarrassment all but saturated her. "No," she repeated in what she hoped was a far more subdued voice.

She heard him laugh softly, and a warmth bathed over her.

"If you don't want to talk to your mother that much, you can always take the phone off the hook," he told her. "Although I wouldn't advise it, because she'll probably catch up to you sooner than later, and in my experience, it's best to deal with things head-on, even if you'd rather avoid them."

Was that a veiled message about her approach to things?

Stop it, stop reading into things. Just be happy he called.

"I don't want to talk about my mother," Mikki told him.

"All right," Jeff responded gamely, "we can talk about something else."

It sounded as if he was leaving the choice of subject up to her. She didn't want to say anything that might wind up pushing her back to square one, so she asked about the first thing she could think of, even though she was afraid that she might accidentally bring up a sore subject.

At this point, she was totally unsure of herself—but not saying anything was even worse, so she began slowly. "How did the party go?"

"Party?" He'd been all but counting the minutes until he felt he could safely call her again. For the last few days—for the first time since he'd started in this field—it was all he could do to keep things going at work. What for him had always been a labor of love had been strictly labor since he had left her house on Sunday. His mind kept wandering back to thoughts of Mikki at the most inopportune times, causing him to lose track of things.

Work had taken a complete back seat in his thoughts. Consequently, he drew a total blank at her question.

"The fiftieth-anniversary party at your restaurant on Sunday," Mikki prompted. Had it gone badly for some reason? Had she raised a subject he would have rather left alone? She felt as if she was verbally all thumbs.

"Oh, that." How could he have forgotten the Strausses' anniversary celebration? Pulling it off had been a huge deal, and he had outdone himself. "That went well. Very well," he told her, adding, "The couple was totally surprised."

Now it was her turn to be confused. "They didn't know they'd been married fifty years?"

He laughed, and the sound went straight to her stomach, causing it to really tighten this time. She'd forgotten how much she really loved the sound of his laugh. Just hearing it was immensely comforting.

"No, they knew," he told her. "But what they didn't know was that their kids were throwing them a big party. The Strausses thought they were just being taken out for dinner."

She could picture the couple entering the large banquet room and the surprise on their faces when they saw that everyone they loved was in that room, celebrating them. That was a family scene she had longed for her whole life.

"Sounds nice," she told him, a wistful note in her voice.

"It was." Jeff paused for a moment, as if debating whether or not to say the next thing. He didn't want to risk scaring Mikki off, but keeping away from her like this was really getting to him. He decided to go for it. "Mikki, could I come over?"

Her heart practically did a backflip. She hadn't ruined it. He wanted to see her.

Almost afraid that this was too good to be true, she asked, "You mean tonight?"

"Yes—unless you want to go slower," he qualified.

Mikki had wanted to see him even before her mother's phone call had gotten her thinking that she had made a huge mistake. She had behaved in a manner that she had always detested—she'd been cowardly. Her fear of giving her heart away and having it broken could have very well cost her the experience of a lifetime: love.

When Jeff had called just now, she had been debating calling him—and praying that he wouldn't just hang up.

Having him ask to come over was an answer to a prayer.

"No, no, tonight's fine," Mikki told him, hoping she didn't sound too eager. She didn't know if that would make him step back.

Just then the doorbell rang.

Why now, she thought. Of all the times she didn't want to see someone...

Determined to tell whoever was there to either go away, or that she'd get back to them, Mikki made her way across the room.

"Hold on, there's someone at the door," she told Jeff. Reaching the door, she closed one eye and looked through the peephole with the other.

"I know," Jeff said. He completed his sentence just as she opened the door. "It's me."

She knew she'd been the one to put up the boundaries, the one who had honestly thought she'd wanted to go slow, but right at this moment, none of that mattered or held true.

Rather than hang back or maintain decorum, or even express surprise at seeing him on her doorstep, Mikki skipped right over that and went straight to throwing her arms around his neck.

Before he could say a single word of greeting, she was kissing him.

Kissing him with all the pent-up passion she'd been denying, passion that had been brewing within her for the last few days and was now tottering on the very brink of release.

Jeff kissed her back, relieved that she wasn't standing on ceremony or telling him that she still wanted him to keep his distance.

Relieved to just be holding her like this again.

And then, just for a moment, he drew back and looked down into her eyes. "I'm sorry, is this what you meant by 'slow'?"

He'd scared her just now. She'd thought that he'd suddenly changed his mind and realized that he'd rather be without her after all. When she saw he was only teasing, she could have cried.

Instead, she raised herself back up on her toes, her heated body pressed urgently against his. "Shut up and kiss me!"

"Yes, ma'am," he answered dutifully, amusement dancing in his eyes. "But I think we should close the door first before your neighbors start talking about the hot doctor who lives at 2712 Mayfair Circle."

The very suggestion of that happening made Mikki start to laugh. Laugh so hard at the image he'd created of gossiping neighbors that it caused every drop of tension that had invaded her body to totally dissipate and disappear.

The sound was infectious, and Jeff wound up laughing right along with her.

Mikki relaxed. It felt wonderful to laugh, and even more wonderful to have Jeff standing here, in her house, being part of her life.

Regaining some of her composure, Mikki finally locked the door. Turning back toward Jeff, she asked, "Can I get you anything?"

He shook his head, almost amused by her question. "I just spent an entire day at the restaurant. I didn't come here to eat, Mikki. I came to find out if I could start seeing you again or if you still wanted me to go slower."

Since it had been eating away at her, she had to ask. "Is that why you didn't come with your mother when she came in for her postsurgical checkup?"

He was honest with her. "I thought if I brought her, you'd think I was using my mother's condition as an excuse to see you."

Mikki shook her head, reviewing the myriad thoughts that had gone through her head when Sophia came in, accompanied by her daughter rather than Jeff. She couldn't remember ever being that disappointed before—not even when her parents had divorced.

She debated keeping that to herself, but then she decided if this relationship was going to work, it had to be based on honesty. No more hiding emotionally for self-preservation purposes.

"When your sister brought your mother in instead of you, I thought I was never going to see you again."

"I was just trying to do what I thought you wanted me to do," he told her simply. Jeff studied her face now, fighting the strong urge to pull her back into his arms. But he needed to get some things cleared up before he could allow himself to move forward. "What *do* you want me to do?"

She didn't want to waste any more precious time. "I want you to forget everything I said before. I want us to go forward."

This was a complete 180 from the wishes she'd expressed when he'd been here the last time. It sounded too good to be true, and that had him feeling just slightly leery.

"Why the change of heart?" he asked her. "What happened?"

"My mother's getting married," Mikki told him bluntly.

He tried to remember what she'd told him when she'd mentioned her mother's unions the last time. "This is husband number five?"

"Maybe six," she allowed.

And then he remembered. "Right, the possible annulment." But why had her mother's pending marriage made her change her feelings about commitment? "Help me out here. Aren't all your mother's marriages the reason why you wanted me to back off?"

Mikki flushed. "Yes."

He shook his head, still not able to make sense out of the change in her attitude. "I'm confused."

She tried her best to explain what she was feeling. "When my mother called to tell me she was getting married and to invite me to the wedding, I finally confronted her and asked why she was going through this again, especially since we both know that her track record when it comes to marriage is less than stellar. Why get married if there's the very real possibility that she'll just divorce this one, too?"

It was a legitimate question. So far, he followed her. "What was her answer?"

"She said that if she didn't keep on trying, then she'd never be able to find the happiness she was hoping for. That she knew it wasn't just going to fall in her lap. And that this latest guy to enter the marital sweepstakes just might be the one. As long as that possibility existed, she was going to go for it."

Jeff laughed shortly. "You know, in its own way, that makes sense," he told her. "If you don't try, you don't stand a chance of winning."

She looked up at him, her eyes meeting his. "I know," she replied.

He ran the back of his hand along her cheek. "You know what else?"

She could feel desire spiking within her. "What?" she asked almost breathlessly.

"You're not your mother. You haven't been frantically going through men, trying to find Mr. Right behind every rock and tree. You've been much too busy, saving the world one patient at a time."

It was a wonderful thing to say, but she knew he wasn't into empty flattery. What was he basing this on? "How would you know?"

"I looked you up," he told her simply. Seeing the surprised look on her face, he quickly assured her, "I wasn't trying to spy on you. I just thought that the more I knew about you, the better my chances were of winning you over."

He touched on a couple of the highlights he'd learned. "You have an awful lot of accolades written about you, not to mention that you've gotten a lot of awards for your 'selfless service,' I think the wording was."

She nodded. That was all well and good, and once upon a time, that had been enough.

But not anymore.

Not after she'd met him. "None of that matters when I come home to an empty house night after night."

"They say pets help fill up the emptiness," he told her, doing his best to keep a straight face.

Seeing the glimmer in his eye, Mikki doubled up her small fist and punched his arm.

"Wow, you have a violent streak. Who knew?" he teased.

And then he kissed her long and hard. When he drew back, he saw the look of surprise on her face. Jeff wasn't finished reviewing the ground rules, because this time around, he wanted to get it right.

"So, if I promise to go very, very slow, can we start seeing each other again? *Really* start seeing each other again?"

"I don't know," she answered, and for a moment, he thought he was back on shaky ground again—until he heard her ask, "Just how slow is slow?"

Drawing her into his arms, he smiled at her. "As slow as you want."

"What if I don't want to go slow at all?"

"Even better," he answered, tightening his arms around her.

There was a look he could only describe as mischievous in her eyes as she asked, "Does this mean that you'll make love with me tonight?"

He was already pressing a kiss to the side of her neck, igniting her. "Twist my arm."

"Why would I ever do that?" she breathed, tugging at his shirt and unbuttoning it.

"Beats me," he replied, the words all but burning along her skin.

"Only if you stop," she warned.

"Then I'd say we've got nothing to worry about," he told her as his lips covered hers again, taking what was already his.

Epilogue

"Well, ladies," Theresa Manetti told her two best friends happily, "this is one more in our plus column."

Theresa slipped into the pew next to Maizie and Cilia after double-checking with her staff to make sure that Mikki and Jeff's specially designed wedding cake would be arriving at Jeff's restaurant in plenty of time for the reception. She had put her best pastry chefs on the job.

"You mean two more, don't you?" Cilia asked. She glanced knowingly in Maizie's direction.

Totally in the dark, Theresa questioned, "Two? Maizie, what is she talking about?"

This was a topic for future discussion, not in church right before the wedding ceremony was about to begin. Maizie's expression was one of pure innocence as she said, "I really have no idea."

Theresa thought otherwise. She turned her attention to Cilia. "Tell me," she ordered.

"Apparently, our friend has taken it upon herself to freelance without telling us." Cilia's smile was triumphant. "You forget," she told Maizie, "our daughters talk."

"Well, *somebody* talk," Theresa insisted. She hated being kept in the dark.

"All right," Maizie relented. "My daughter came to me after talking to Mikki to see how things were going. She was afraid Mikki was never going to risk getting married no matter how wonderful Jeff was—not until her mother finally found someone stable she could really settle down with. If that happened, that would encourage Mikki to say yes to Jeff."

"And so Maizie found someone for her," Cilia said, taking over the narrative. "Honestly, Maizie, sometimes you just talk too slowly—the wedding's almost starting."

"Wait," Theresa interrupted, still trying to get the story straight. "So you played matchmaker for Mikki's mother?" she asked Maizie. "Without us?"

Maizie nodded. "I'm afraid I did," she confessed. "I knew a gentleman who was just perfect for her mother—and Nikki helped," she added proudly.

"Nikki? Your daughter, Nikki?" Theresa questioned, surprised.

"The apple doesn't fall all that far from the tree," Cilia told their friend.

Maizie quickly filled her friends in. "Randolph is a retired army doctor. Kind, intelligent and not the type to be intimidated by a forceful woman. I think he's just the influence that Veronica needs in her life. Her mother marrying Randolph also showed Mikki that the right one *can* come along if you don't give up. And Lord knows, that woman never gave up."

Theresa laughed softly. "My, the lengths we go to in order to help our unsuspecting clients find happiness," she marveled.

"Well, it worked," Maizie said proudly. "The happy couple had their reception at Jeff's restaurant. And during the celebration, Jeff worked up his nerve to propose to Mikki." Maizie's smile went right to her eyes. "I hear tell that she couldn't say yes fast enough."

"You are one devious woman, Maizie Sommers," Cilia told her friend.

Maizie exchanged glances with her two friends. "We all are." Then, before either one of them could say anything in response to her comment, she said, "Shh. It's starting."

A moment later, Cilia looked at her closely. "Maizie, you're tearing up."

"Nikki is her matron of honor," she pointed out. "Isn't she beautiful?"

"Always," Theresa and Cilia both agreed, although it wasn't clear if Maizie was talking about her daughter or the latest young bride.

Right about now, she'd expected to be nervous—to the point that she would be contemplating bolting from the church. Instead, Mikki realized that she had never felt more confident in her life. Marrying Jeff, committing herself for the rest of her life to this man, was not just the right thing to do, she knew that it was the *only* thing to do.

And here she was, slowly walking down the aisle toward the man of her dreams.

She couldn't believe it.

And to think that she had almost thrown it all away out of fear because she didn't want to emulate her mother's mistakes.

Mikki glanced over to where her mother was seated with her new husband. Her *last* new husband, her mother had whispered when she'd introduced Randolph to Mikki, and she'd felt her mother actually meant it. More important, she felt that this man was going to keep her mother happy.

Love was possible in this turbulent world, Mikki thought happily—and *she* had found her love. Thank goodness he hadn't given up on her.

As she slowly made her way down the aisle behind her best friend, her eyes were focused on the man at the altar. The man who had been patient enough to wait out her craziness.

The man she was meant to be with forever.

When she finally reached the altar and joined Jeff before the minister, Jeff leaned in and whispered to her, "You came," as if he had been harboring some doubts.

Mikki smiled warmly at him. "Wouldn't have missed this for the world," she whispered back.

And then they both turned to look at the minister, who began to say the words that would, in the end, join them for the rest of their lives.

The way they were meant to be.

* * * * *

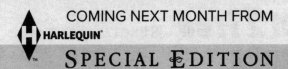

Before Lila could ask any more questions, she suddenly
found herself looking up at Everett. The fund-raiser was
a black-tie affair and Everett was wearing the obligatory
tuxedo.

It was at that moment that Lila realized Everett in a tuxedo
was even more irresistible than Everett wearing scrubs.

Face it, the man would be irresistible even wearing a kilt.

"What are you doing here?" Lila asked when she finally
located her tongue and remembered how to use it.

"You know, we're going to have to work on getting you
a new opening line to say every time you see me," Everett
told her with a laugh. "But to answer your question, I was
invited."

Lucie stepped up with a slightly more detailed explanation
to her friend's question. "The invitation was the foundation's
way of saying thank you to Everett for his volunteer work."

"Disappointed to see me?" he asked Lila. There was a touch of humor in his voice, although he wasn't quite sure just what to make of the stunned expression on Lila's face.

"No, of course not," Lila denied quickly. "I'm just surprised, that's all. I thought you were still back in Houston."

"I was," Everett confirmed. "The invitation was express mailed to me yesterday. I thought it would be rude to ignore it, so here I am," he told her simply, as if all he had to do was teleport himself from one location to another instead of drive over one hundred and seventy miles.

"Here you are," Lila echoed.

Everything inside her was smiling and she knew that was a dangerous thing. Because when she was in that sort of frame of mind, she tended not to be careful. And that was when mistakes were made.

Mistakes with consequences.

She was going to have to be on her guard, Lila silently warned herself. And it wasn't going to be easy being vigilant, not when Everett looked absolutely bone-meltingly gorgeous the way he did.

As if his dark looks weren't already enough, Lila thought, the tuxedo made Everett look particularly dashing.

You're not eighteen anymore, remember? Lila reminded herself. *You're a woman. A woman who has to be very, very careful.*

She just hoped she could remember that.

Don't miss
THE FORTUNE MOST LIKELY TO...
by Marie Ferrarella, available March 2018 wherever
Harlequin® Special Edition books and ebooks are sold.

www.Harlequin.com

LOVE
Harlequin
romance?

Join our Harlequin community to share your thoughts and connect with other romance readers!

Be the first to find out about promotions, news, and exclusive content!

Sign up for the Harlequin e-newsletter and download a free book from any series at

www.TryHarlequin.com

CONNECT WITH US AT:

Harlequin.com/Community

 Facebook.com/HarlequinBooks

 Twitter.com/HarlequinBooks

 Instagram.com/HarlequinBooks

 Pinterest.com/HarlequinBooks

ReaderService.com

**ROMANCE WHEN
YOU NEED IT**

HSOCIAL2017

THE WORLD IS BETTER WITH

Romance

Harlequin has everything from contemporary, passionate and heartwarming to suspenseful and inspirational stories.

Whatever your mood, we have a romance just for you!

Connect with us to find your next great read, special offers and more.

f /HarlequinBooks

@HarlequinBooks

www.HarlequinBlog.com

www.Harlequin.com/Newsletters

HARLEQUIN®

A *Romance* FOR EVERY MOOD™

www.Harlequin.com

SERIESHALOAD2015

Earn points from all your Harlequin book purchases from wherever you shop.

Turn your points into *FREE BOOKS* of your choice
OR
EXCLUSIVE GIFTS from your favorite authors or series.

Join for FREE today at
www.HarlequinMyRewards.com.

Harlequin My Rewards is a free program (no fees) without any commitments or obligations.

MYR17